Rice Pudding in a Duvet

Acknowledgements

I would like to express my thanks to Annemarie at Mill House Publishers for her kind encouragement and wise words, and Emma at Sivellink for her delightful inspiration and skill with the front cover art-work of this the second edition. Finally, huge hugs to my Family. They put up with many a substandard meal, all while I was absorbed with writing a book inspired by delicious food.

With love,

Heather.

In memory of Jessica

Rice Pudding in a Duvet

a journey home with snacks

Heather Gartside

We plant a tree
for every book sold

Paperback
ISBN 978-8792632-91-3

Cover art by Sivellink www.sivellink.dk

Illustrations 2017 © D.W. Designs

All characters in this publication are fictitious; resemblance to any persons living or dead is purely coincidental

Mill House publishers, Denmark
www.millhouse-publishers.com

Contents

Prologue

Dear Kirsty,

My eldest child - in a little while you'll leave your funny old mum and head out in the world to college. It must sound like a cliché, but it feels like only yesterday that I was doing the same and waving goodbye to my mother; always goodbyes and long distances. Tomorrow it's time for my own baby bird to flex her stubby wings and take the first journey to another branch. I'll watch you go, hide my tears and smile. Then, when you return I'll make you tea with ginger and you'll never know that I've thought so much about you. You'll be standing proud, tall and different before me, I'll be a little greyer, a little wiser, so very glad to see you, and a little lost for words. So after tea I'll cook for you and pour all the ingredients of my love into that meal, secretly waiting for your gourmet approval and to see your little nose twitch.

You'll have a hundred things to do once your bags are unpacked in your new college dorm, so put this little book by your bed to tell you an alternative bedtime story before you sleep. I hope it will make you smile to read this collection that I've been tapping away at for the past couple of years. It has all those best recipes that you've grown up with, and also the stories of all the silly, risqué and downright dangerous things that I used to get up to when I tasted those delicacies for the first time. I know that I'm a bit of an unconventional mum, and it feels like it's time that you knew about what a twit I've been at times. Just remember that my heart came home to you the minute you began to grow inside me. And I thank you for the miracle of you, my little "Pip."

Before you go, there are a couple of other things I've realised along the way that I'd like to share:

1. *Be nice. You are a nice person, never let people lessen that in you. Just keep shining and all the people that you wish in your life will come your way. It will save you a lot of time and energy if you don't try to be tough and hard, too slim or behaving like someone else. Be your very own lovely self!*

2. *And whenever shit happens, as it does from time to time, just remember that all those absolutely awful moments and all those brilliant adventures you have will make great stories for your future children one day!*

Enjoy and experience it all. It's your own delicious feast - just invite me over for a snack sometime!

From your loving mum,

Alice Bonneville-Beck

1. French Tart

September 1992

I had begun my once illustrious, now ridiculous, rise to fame and riches when I was five years old. One sunny 1960s afternoon, while helping my granny to make an apple pie, I'd asked her,

'How do I get in the jet set?'

'Oh, I don't bloody know, Alice,' she snorted. 'I wouldn't be making apple pies if I did, but if you find out then I'm coming too!'

In those few words she sowed the seeds of curiosity and a burning ambition. It lay camouflaged for twenty-four years, waiting for my chance to strike gold. I struck rock bottom of course, as no self respecting jet-setter gains the golden ticket without selling their soul. I even succeeded in buckling my seatbelt, and took a short and acutely painful journey in the company of fellow jet-setters. In retrospect, I rather wished that I'd stuck to making apple pies, realising that it wasn't for me by the time I reached the departure lounge, but by then my ticket was booked.

The luxury brand company that head-hunted me had its headquarters in Paris. The day that Madame Sécheresse telephoned me from the agency representing the company, I was caught unawares and hadn't a clue about the firm that she was referring to. Flattered immensely at them noticing me and sniffing a fast buck in the air, I quickly took a metro journey to the Champs Élysées to checkout who they were and what they sold. They fitted all the jet-set requirements with their vulgar products, powerless portrayal of women and worship of all that money could buy.

With the HIV crisis in full swing, I had twice gained employment in the bow-tying world of display and decoration work, partially because of all the tragic vacancies left by my predecessors. Here I was again, a robust young woman with no fear of heights sitting at a huge desk with one drawer thoughtlessly still filled with snapshots of islands in Thailand and discos in New York City. I closed the drawer sadly and wondered how on earth I'd passed the Human Resources examination. But then I'd decided to sell my soul and make big money; admittedly I was only 5 years old when I fancied the idea the first time.

My office was situated on the seventeenth floor of the Grande Arche de la Dèfense. As I climbed the gleaming white stairs that led me under the towering building, I had the distinct feeling I was in a Busby Berkeley musical, and a gaggle of high-kicking spangle-studded male dancers would grab me and transport me to the elevator whilst I lay on their outstretched arms. As my spectral accomplices transported me skywards, I knew, again, in my heart that it was a world that was so not suited to this curious girl who rather liked singing to sheep; but there were similarities. It was too late and became a classic case of the show must go on, regardless of the production price.

From day one I spent most of my time sitting on the toilet. I was the good-looking global manager of bow-tying, but I was acting my heart out. I sat queasily behind the dead man's desk with a very large mobile phone in hand, and looked to the entire world like I'd won the lottery. How scared I was though, I lost four kilos of pure fear in the first week.

Other than pretending to be someone else, I did have many other fabulous and extraordinary experiences. I often felt my Grandmother's spirit at my side, as she wafted in with me through the revolving doors and velvet curtains of the top hotels of the world. Finally, at the tail end of the twentieth century it had happened; a fine mist of perfume completed the illusion and crystal champagne flutes chinked, then passed to our bloodied giggling lips.

One day I was summoned to Munich to help install a gala promotion of bow-tying. Anyone who was anyone from the German social elite was gathered for this *Spectacle* arranged by a well known French theatre producer. I attended to my jobs and eyed the rehearsals on the catwalk; a supermodel stalked sulkily holding a whip in her gauntleted talons, I wondered what other masterpieces of mise-en-scène would follow?

Later that day, when all the shrieking and frenzy of the preparations had subsided, I joined the perfumed VIPs to drink champagne and take in the show. The standing crowd swayed to the ministrations of handsome waiters, hushing as the band struck up with a Can-Can. I cringed as six well-built girls cartwheeled down the catwalk dressed in French maid costumes complete with bobbed hair, huge false eyelashes and pink feather dusters. The handsome and half pissed Germans cheered enthusiastically at all the flesh and innuendoes, topping up their glasses and sniggering at the predictability of their French hosts. Next came the supermodel, this time leading a very frightened baby giraffe and both clad in leopard-print leather. She sashayed her beautiful South London self to the sound of jungle drums and monkey calls. The politically incorrect French had truly surpassed themselves. Female VIPs whispered acerbically behind invisible fans as if in a Georgian salon, and aroused men rolled aching tongues across the floor for the goddess to pierce her leopard print stilettos through.

A kindly looking waiter passed by and I gestured for him to keep the champagne flowing my way. We winked conspiratorially and I felt the designer bubbles begin to make me braver than I really was. The next act was announced with a drum roll and an impressive resonance of real didgeridoos. Two young kangaroos, with designer boxing gloves on, pounded their powerful way all over the catwalk. Four French maids, now bedecked in suits reminiscent of aboriginal body painting, restrained the flailing beasts. The act was quickly over, the audience cheered and the French maids bent over exposing their pert bottoms and cleared the kangaroo shit up. Lastly, the entire cast came in for a round of bowing and self congratulation. I took another drink.

After the final applause dwindled into a hum of conversation, the orchestra collected their instruments and exited the pit. In their place came a small ensemble with clarinet, harmonica, fiddle, ukulele, trombone and piano. With no introduction, the six earnest young men began to play the Charleston. Granny and I were in flapper heaven.

It was impossible not to start dancing. Once I began, so did my immediate neighbours, dropping any inhibitions that the champagne hadn't stripped away already and joining me in a hilarious improvised celebration. Mind you, the bulk of the crowd held back and enjoyed the sight of us all making whoopee. With insane grins on our faces and feeling pretty sure that we were brilliant at it, we continued playing criss-cross with our knees and waving our hands around. Suddenly, I was grabbed from behind; a big handsome bear of a man in a tuxedo twirled me around and left me gasping and giggling at the end of his outstretched arm like we were Fred and Ginger.

The band struck up again with *Steamboat Shuffle* and my masterful German and I twirled and shimmied to our hearts content. Not content with remaining with the audience, my ambitious dancing partner dragged me to the foot of the catwalk. I tried to lead him off it, but he was drunk on success and disastrously determined.

The clarinets wailed and we were living the dream. Well, he was. All eyes and then spotlights were on us in the huge auditorium, including the emergency services that had a stretcher and medics waiting nearby. My determined German was perspiring. He swiftly twirled me around one last time and fell backwards off the two metre high catwalk. I screamed, then fell right on top of his big sausage-gobbling paunch. The room gasped and the stretcher bearers ran forward.

The paparazzi arrived at the same time as the medics. I came off unscathed physically, but was suffering from mortification about the scandal and the possibility of losing my job. All these thoughts went through my jangling mind, while I lay on top of the flattened German whilst the happy cameras flashed. My dancing partner was extracted by laughing colleagues and disappeared, no doubt with internal injuries caused by 70 kilos of flying squirrel.

My boss whisked me off to my hotel room in a limousine, trying to suppress the scandal of one of their employees squashing a captain of German industry and upstaging a notoriously stroppy supermodel.

I slept like a milk-sated baby in the softest and downiest bed in world, oblivious to the machinations of the press and PR departments. Refreshed, I descended to the hotel foyer in the morning to be greeted with all my colleagues cheering and more cameras flashing.

On the flight back to Paris I was seated next to the illustrious theatre producer. We said good morning politely and then I asked when he wanted me to start work?

'*Jamais!*' He laughed, casually handing me the German *Hello* magazine with yours truly plastered all over it.

Recipe for French Chocolate Tart

My first thought of a recipe to accompany this tale was of a sorbet of foie gras. My youngest daughter asked me what that was and I explained that it was pâté ice cream. We both decided that it sounded like a very bad idea, but then the best ideas seldom come when too much money is being flashed around. Instead, I offer you a French tart, I must have looked like one that night.

This is a tantalising chocolate tart. Best to make the pastry case in advance and attend to the filling just before your guests arrive, wearing fancy lingerie of course.

First make the pastry. Sift 450g plain flour, 150g icing sugar, a pinch of sea salt and the seeds scraped from a vanilla pod. Rub in 225g butter, then mix to a dough with the addition of 1 egg and I tablespoon of milk. Roll out the pastry, line a suitable (approx 24 cm) flan dish and chill the rolled dough for about 30 minutes before you bake it. There will be too much pastry left over, so roll another flan case out and freeze it for a rainy day. Pre-heat the oven to 180°C / 350 °F / Gas 4 and bake the flan case for about 15 minutes, or until gently browned. To make the filling first whisk 3 eggs, 1 egg yolk and 100g sugar together until light and doubled in volume. Turn the oven down to 150°C / 300°F / Gas 2. Melt 350g good quality plain chocolate, 50g butter, 25ml cream and 50g of Armagnac together in a *bain marie.* Fold in the egg mixture until well blended. Pour this into the cooked pastry case and bake in the oven for about 20 minutes, or until firm to the touch. Serve the flan garnished with a few small fragments of (fake) gold leaf and bend over showing your fancy underwear when you remove it from the oven.

2. Baby Potatoes in Sea Salt

July 1974

Epic adventure holidays were the foundation stones of my childhood, and the base from which I eventually sprang into a nomadic future. The desire to travel and explore held religious status within the Bonneville houschold, and my father would spend many months pouring over road maps; fine-tuning the destination and adding points of historical interest along the way, all rather like a chef planning a banquet. It wasn't the destination that was the centrepiece anyway, it was the journey - with snacks!

Spain was invariably the sunny destination, it ticked all the boxes for high points of historical and geographical interest; stunning landscapes, a population that loved us children, wonderful food, cheap prices, glorious weather - and it exercised dad's dubious command of the Spanish language,

'I wanto petrolio!'

He slowly mouthed, as he waved an empty Sainsbury's orange squash container at a bemused Spanish forecourt attendant with a mad look in his eyes. Despite our French sounding name, we were descended from the conquering Normans of 1066, and dad lacked the inclination to speak foreign languages after being on an island for a thousand years.

Meanwhile, my brother Ben, mum and I sat a couple of kilometres away, baked with aniseed in the midday sun by a highway in Castille. The dusty Ford Cortina ticking hotly to the accompaniment of balefully howling dogs.

Despite his obliqueness, he would always raise a smile and get himself understood by the local inhabitants. dad was instinctively in full possession of all the knowing guile and enjoyable charisma of a true traveller. With a full plastic container in hand, he'd return as a shifting mirage on the parched road. The strong legs and swinging gait suggested a man in his stride returning triumphant to his beautiful wife, and us kids fat from all those sugary drinks. The litre of orange scented gasoline generally providing just enough energy for the lurching car to reach the garage again, and for us all to meet his confused new amigo.

For dad and I food was a wondrous highlight to their three vivid weeks spent beyond the grey English Channel. For mum, cooking was to be endured but she'd much prefer not to and dine out. Consequently, a full supply of tinned British provisions were a 'must have' for the perilous journey through France.

A forty year old Alice opens the kitchen cutlery drawer in my home in Denmark and extracts a tin opener. I stroke the shiny handles, wondering as I always do why the cutting part looked a bit rusty. Then, smiling I recall how it was mother's cooking utensil of preference, and with this firmly grasped in her strong hands she had set about the bleak prospect of their first campsite meal all those years ago in Northern France.

We would take a Channel ferry from Southampton to Cherbourg, trying to avoid the British Rail *Sealink* ferries (referred to by dad as *Seastink*) which plied the route to the monotonously devastated Pas de Calais. My brother Ben was thirteen, an avid reader of *Sven Hassel* nazi war novels, and an authority on all things gruesome from WW2. The Cherbourg peninsula provided abundant access to grisly wartime sites, and in the 1970s these were still relatively intact from all the recent atrocities. Our family happily sped past the remaining tank traps and weed strewn battlefields to *Camping La Manche.*

A quick blast of crap French, with a Lancashire accent from dad,

'Avez vous le camping pour moi, monsieur?'

To the enthusiastic and madly gesticulating retort of a patron amazed that an Englishman could actually speak his language,

'Oui, nous avons beaucoup de places pour vous, monsieur. C'est vraiment un plaisir de vous accueillir.'

To which my bluffing father replied with a lavish shoulder shrug, outstretched palms and flying eyebrows, then letting loose a lavishly reverberating fart sound from his pouting lips.

There were certain procedures to adhere to when setting-up the Bonneville family tent when in continental Europe:

1. Set the camp up before the Germans.
2. Try and expose as little flesh as possible in the communal bathrooms.
3. Pitch the tent relatively close to the bathrooms, as 'our Alice' is always peeing in the night.
4. Camp far enough away not to have to watch the French all taking their plastic toilet buckets in the morning. (I secretly dreamed of owning a bucket of my own)
5. Keep an eye on what Ben "finds" on his forays.
6. Don't respond to what the neighbours are cooking.

As soon as the tent was extracted from the car, the family sprang into action like they were part of a travelling circus. dad and Ben were occupied with erecting the tent and pegging it in securely enough to withstand a hurricane. While mum stealthily selected her lethal tins of *Fray Bentos Stewed Steak*, dead green beans and a jar of mealy boiled potatoes. With a grim look on her face she rotated the mechanism on the tin opener, and deposited the combined dog food into an aluminium saucepan. It was devastatingly bad.

I wandered back from the *lavabos* with my two gallon squash bottle full of water and a baguette from the camp shop. It was part of my job to check-out the toilet facilities. I'd seen, with a groan, that there were only the 'hole in the ground' type of WC's that resembled showers and forced you to vulnerably hover, wee on your feet and assume that French plumbers were women haters. The final piece of reconnaissance certified that the washrooms communal.

'The French ladies were spraying a lot of perfume on and not washing much, and the German ladies were washing hands, face und zumting else very vigorously!' I noted. Mother wouldn't be happy.

A young Alice staggered along the sandy path and passed a gleaming new tent, where a petite French housewife wearing a pretty apron and pointy bra lovingly tended to the *plat du jour.* The soft sizzle and whisper of frying onions; the seductive vapours curling into my twitching nostrils and a forbidden sideways glance as the woman lingeringly coaxed dark red saucisson into the hot *Le Creuset* pan.

Returning to the Bonneville camping pitch, I spied our colossally large and faded tent erected, with four plates of steaming dog food placed on the rickety camping table, and dad sadly pouring himself a large melamine beaker of *Vin de table* from a bottle with stars around the top. Offering him the bread he smiled sweetly, and we turned and sniffed the breeze blowing from the direction of the French tent. On the plus side the meal was over quickly and thrown into *la poubelle*, only the exquisitely crisp and salty baguette was demolished with a bit of out-of-place cheddar, and mum and dad happily getting stuck into the rough wine and breaking into the occasional song.

After supper I occupied myself with counting the rabbit poos that were liberally scattered all over the grass, then discovering some very impressive holes that led into a warren stretching far beyond some barbed wire, and towards the sand dunes and roaring sea. Hung on the wire was an old sign that said, *Défense d'entrer* and another with *Terrain de manœuvre* with a faded skull and crossbones. But my quest for the gallic cousin's of Pipkin and Bigwig from *Watership Down* led me further on, under the wire and down the first marram grass covered sand dune. Ben looked up from reading about Sven Hassel slitting Russian soldiers throats in Stalingrad, sensing a potential mission with his gullible little sister as the scapegoat on her search for bunny poo. Checking to see that our parents had dozed off and were dribbling, he dived under the wire and feigned interest in my impressive excavation of a sizeable chunk of the warren.

'Look, more rabbit holes over there!' indicated Ben to a briar patch in the lee of another large dune.

'More bunnies,' I gaily chortled and happily followed Ben over the fine sand, unbeknown to us riddled with landmines from the 1940s. At the crest of this sand dune we surveyed the terrain and spied a rusted tank trapped in a ravine.

'That looks like a M4A2 Sherman tank' said Ben impassively.

'It was nicknamed "Donald Duck" because it was amphibious and floated onto the Normandy landing beaches from the cruisers further out to sea' he knowledgeably added.

'Let's go and have a closer look!' and 'Oh look, a bunny rabbit!' for maximum effect on nine-year old me.

The ploy worked once again, and we spent many a happy hour playing around the tank and never once wondering at the violent happenings attached to the site, or finding a rabbit family.

Ben and I wandered over the restricted area, and the setting sun signalled that our reconnaissance time was up in *Sven-Hassel-Land.*

Ben stumbled upon three bronze mortar cartridges, still in their casings and his for the plucking. He took two, and kindly handed me the third live bomb.

Sharing is caring! I happily mused.

'Hmm, looks like a M49A3 High Explosive Cartridge with Super-Quick Point Detonating fuze M525 to me' muttered Ben indulgently. 'Let's take them back to the campsite and defuse them in the morning.'

'Sounds like fun,' I chirped.

Us two young explorers, thrilled and complete with live ammunition lodged under our arms, scrambled back to the tent to enjoy some tinned rice pudding in a sleeping bag. The sun set magnificently in the west and the sound of zips and muttering in surrounded tents signalled the end of the day.

The Bonneville family lived to pack away the camp, and as I wandered off to wee in the marram grass at dawn I spotted Ben and joined him to diffuse and stash the mortars in the chassis of the Cortina. After a breakfast we headed south as grey skies urged us onwards, the rabbits once again reclaiming the beaches and occasionally getting blown to smithereens.

'Look Mummy, red roofs!' I squeaked from the backseat of the tightly packed car as Normandy became the Val de Loire.

Ben looked up from reading about the WW2 German construction of the Atlantic wall by slave labour, and casually picked a bogey and ate it. The terracotta tiles signified moving south, so he reluctantly put his D-Day books away and retrieved some pamphlets from his satchel about the nazi collaboration of the interim French Vichy government.

We camped by lazy willow lined rivers, inhaling the musk of old pebbles and spraying ourselves liberally in DDT. Later, after a tin of *Sainsbury's Chunky Chicken in White Sauce* we wandered the streets of ancient towns, as swallows blazed past in the setting sunlight over warm pavements and the ancient bell of church tolled 9pm.

Every few days we drove for two four-hour stretches, and I muttered under my breath a modified song from Cher,

> *'I was born in the wagon of a travelling show,*
> *My mamma used to dance for the money they'd throw,*
> *Papa would do whatever he could.'*

Then repeat.

After about 1000 mantra rounds I'd hear my parents discussing the merits of likely picnic spots, followed by the blissful sound of descending gears and the decisive halt of the motor. We'd spend long lunch hours napping in the shade of huge trees, with a bottle of wine tied with string around the neck and cooling in trout-filled streams. Ben would invariably saunter off to the nearest copse and return with a German jackboot, helmet or shard of shrapnel - minus accompanying body parts. The rickety camping table would reappear; folding chairs, melamine plates, a crisp baguette, some nutty Emmental, gloriously malformed tomatoes, olives and the last remnants of English food - salad cream and some orange squash. It wouldn't be long until it was all used up, and dad and I could gleefully slip into charcuterie shops and emerge like Christmas morning clutching waxed boxes of *champignons à la grecque, celeric rémoulade, carrottes râpées, Tomates farçies* and warm *pain de campagne.*

Golden days through the car window continued on our journey south, with snacks. Eventually into the densely forested mountains of the Auvergne, and dad's research on a man-eating wolf from the 17th century began to come alive. *La Bête du Gévaudan,* a wolf-like monster which terrorised the local peasants and caused a national outcry in France at the time. His bedtime horror stories, told in a deep Johnny Cash voice and with the occasional impromptu howl from mum sent both Ben and I into a gleefully petrified sleep.

The cool mountain mist descending upon the flapping canvas tent, our silhouetted family looming large and comical from a hissing gas lamp, and a large red she-wolf paused with ears pricked, then continued to disembowel a whimpering pet Labrador.

Despite the thrills, the joys of camping were beginning to wane and a real bed beckoned much further south, in Spain. The custard coloured Cortina nosed her way towards the Dordogne and the south western reaches of France. Persecuted *Cathars*, walled cities and medieval sanitation mingled juices with corrupt catholics in the vivid historical diatribes that dad has researched over the damp winter in England. The temperatures soared and the sun baked my felt pens into banana shapes in the back window of the car. Damp morning towels were placed on the windows and they flapped to a sweet rhythm which mesmerised me as I chanted,

'Gypsies, tramps with fleas, they call us in the centre of the town.
They call us, gypsies, tramps with fleas,
But every night oh ho, they come and lay their bunny down.'

We took the coastal road into Catalonia, it writhed beside the endless blue as the Pyrenees tumbled into the sea. Not the time to look down as we navigated the tortuous corniche and gingerly emerged on the dry side of the mountains heading for Puerto de la Selva.

The small, white houses of the fishing village nestled into each other, as if to seek shelter together from the ferocious Tramuntana winter wind. An apartment had been booked and proved to be stuffy and a little ramshackle, which I felt was due to the recently deceased (scowling) old lady that kept noticing in the corner of my eye. The marble floors were cool though, the heavy dining table and ornate dresser a welcomed relief from the wobbly camping table, and the well-worn beds with dubious stains were heavenly compared to our inflatable mattresses.We installed ourselves in record time, and were soon tucking into takeaway *pollos asados, patatas fritas, aioli* and the very last trickle of orange squash on the roof of the apartment as the newly arrived German neighbours continued to unpack.

Without the need to up and leave every other day, my family relaxed into the Spanish pattern of sleeping late in the morning and staying out at nighttime. The pebbly beach beckoned to Ben and I, and with newly purchased snorkels we witnessed a silent undersea wonderland of steep canyons, darting fish, starfish and languorously waving seaweed. Whole days were spent diving into the cool sapphire waters, and long evenings spent extracting painful sea urchin quills from our pink feet. This opened up a new pastime, after witnessing French divers extracting the prickly *oursins* with gleaming knives from rocky ledges. And with a jolly,

'Bon appétit,' cutting them open and popping into their glistening mouths.

We invested our pocket money in rubber sandals and penknives engraved with *Cataluña* to wage a campaign against the prickly foe. By the time the week was over we had amassed fifty cleanly scraped shells, which I had plans to add seashell feet and googly eyes to once back in England. Happy days, as we ruthlessly flung the pulsating entrails off the roof terrace to the feral cats in the scrubland below, and with a cheerful whistle continued scalping the now spineless *Echinoidea.*

The week flew past and my parents made a daily visit the local bodega to fill the numerous empty orange squash containers with sugary banana, coffee and nut flavoured liqueurs. Glass *vino de mesa* bottles were filled with *ron* and Fundador brandy from huge oak casks in darkly boozy cellars. They'd return from the outing singing like the family Von Trapp, only Ben sulking contemptuously as I innocently joined in the drunken singalong of snippets from Carmen and Tommy Steele singing *The Little White Bull.*

The sea urchin shells were packed, the snorkels, a doll dressed like a flamenco dancer, the liqueurs, strings of garlic and a new shopping basket thoughtfully placed for mum to put her feet in for the long journey home. dad checked the oil and water, and cleaned the car windscreens. In an inspired moment he inspected the exhaust after hearing an occasional disturbing rattle on the journey south, then discovered three mortar shells lodged in the chassis. Ben denied everything, then said it was me who made him do it.

Recipe for Baby Potatoes in Sea Salt

With the tinned food safely dispatched along the way, Spain was an open hamper in which to forage and delight in with no guilt. My father's command of the Catalan and Spanish languages were almost plausible; as he bridged the political divide smashing schoolboy French with a sprinkling of key Spanish words, and British words with an 'o' on them whenever at a loss for vocabulary.

'Tapas, por favor.' He'd gaily cry and the family would nervously wait for their supper of tripe and fried cod tongues. But I was in junior tastebuds heaven, and couldn't wait to get home in order to study tapas recipes by torchlight late at night in my pink English bedroom. I gave *ensaladilla Rusa* a miss though, finding that it made me feel sick. But this recipe for baby new potatoes cooked slowly in sea salt until they are tender, sweet and ancient to look at, then a gobsmackingly powerful mustardy salsa achingly slapping you on the face - well it etched it's way into my young memory and blew my mind!

The Spanish name for this method of cooking potatoes is papas arrugadas, meaning wrinkly potatoes. Almost a metaphor for life; as a fresh young potato is transformed into a tired and shrivelled looking husk, but is full of the condensed flavour of what it has experienced. Perhaps like me as I recall this today?

Begin the alchemy by placing about 600g of lightly washed, tiny and perfect new potatoes in a frying pan wide and deep enough so that they sit in an even layer. Don't cut the baby potatoes in half, or break the skin as they will absorb too much salt! Pour over about 300g of water and add a hefty tbsp of sea salt. Bring to the boil and simmer gently for 40 mins. When the water begins to evaporate, give the pan a shake to coat the potatoes in the salt. Once the potatoes are covered in a light salty crust, they are ready to serve.

While the baby potatoes are losing their youth to the ravages of sea and sun make the herb salsa. Chop the 2 cloves garlic, 2 big handfuls of fresh flat-leaf parsley, 1 bunch of fresh basil, 1 handful of fresh sage and 1 small handful of capers with a smattering of sweet pickled gherkins. Resist the urge to blitz them in the blender (too fine), but by all means try placing all the salsa ingredients in a beaker and snipping repeatedly with a pair of kitchen scissors for a lovely rough, yet palatable bit of preparation. Add about 2 tablespoons of Dijon mustard, 3 tablespoons red wine vinegar and 8 tablespoons of really good extra virgin olive oil. Check the seasoning - I generally find that there's no need for extra salt. If you want to go the whole way, then add 5 - 6 anchovy fillets. You can serve the potatoes by sticking a cocktail stick in each of them, then drizzling the salsa onto them artistically. Optionally, cut the base off each baby potato and place them on a platter like little standing stones. Spoon the salsa on the top of each one and prepare for the extraordinary mummified taste explosion!

3. Meat and Two Veg

September 1981

School days were an ordeal and I became quite a skiver. But being very creative I was always attentive to the white make-up and warm flannel that I applied in order to trick my mother that I was terribly sick. Or in the scraping of the school report with a razor blade to make E's into B's for maths and science. I was A* in the creative subjects, which made my dummy status at maths unbearable.

After several years of skiving, I arrived at Cheltenham Art College in 1982, sporting a home perm that my mother had thoughtfully done for me. I was eighteen years old and supposed to be a grown-up, but was a lonely child in a teenager wrapping trying to be brave. I went home at the weekends with the pretence of doing my laundry. Once there, I developed the desire to become Minnie the Jack Russell; contentedly sleeping in her basket by the radiator all day, listening to mum's off-key whistling as she ironed or vacuumed, and popping out now and then for windswept walks in the wide-angle russet landscapes of Herefordshire. Those canine longings were pretty weird, even for an art student. But the acute home-sickness and desire to hover around my family home stayed with me for years. Whenever I returned home, tremendous booms, bangs and crashes would sound around the house as soon as I settled down on the sofa for a parental cuddle. Connie, my mum, would be up like a shot jangling with theories:

'Oh, that must have been *Brian Trubshaw* test-flying Concorde! He must have just gone through the sound barrier.'

'David, when will you fix those shelves in our Alice's room? That sounded like all her books falling again!'

Dad would stoically climb the spiral staircase to paranormal activity, and return a nonplussed engineer muttering about earth subsidence and wooden beams contracting as they cooled. I knew it was me though, me and my band of in-house succubus, ghouls and huge-headed sleep snatchers. Why I'd been selected for a nightly hallucinating, haunting and sleeplessness throughout my youth I've never worked out. Mum said that my Granny Bonneville had powers, although I'd only ever seen her once speaking in tongues outside some Norman portcullis in Wales. Dad said that it was because the entrance fee was too dear. So I'd wash my bag of Cheltenham life. Dry it in the sweet country air. Scare the shit out of my parents. Give Minnie's chewed basket a last longing look and return in my Renault 5 weeping into my even more frightening future.

Not far into the second semester of the art foundation course, I managed to find a new flat. It was just what I'd wanted. I clasped my new keys and mounted honeyed limestone steps into my gracious Georgian home. The owner, an ancient retired concert pianist, lived on the ground floor. My room was on the first floor and shined confidently with oval walls, ochre paint, a white ceiling and a dark grey wooden floor. At the far end was a sash window, with a mulberry tree partly hiding the untidy garden. I was inspired and breathless at the simple classical beauty of it. Feeling comfortable and correctly installed, I began my first true descent into bohemian life at record speed. No more doggy beds for me! I wanted Marcel Duchamp and

Radio 4, coffee filtered over chipped enamel mugs, Albert Camus, Johannes Sebastian Bach, strong Belgian beer, Red Stripe cigarettes and very little food. My ridiculous home perm went away and Jean Seberg returned. All I needed was a friend to read my thesaurus with in flickering candlelight.

No matter how many times I'd wind my weary home looking gaunt and ascetic my mother would embrace me, turn the bath on, sigh at my Joan of Arc hairstyle, swiftly hide the doggy bed and serve me with a steaming plate of stewed steak or else chicken soup. I'd let her know months before that I was now a sensitive artist and vegetarian. But to no avail, the steaming dinner was dished-up and on the table.

Recipe for Meat and Two Veg

This recipe is stunningly simple, and I'm sure breaks every culinary rule with its backward marinating, liberal use of *Bisto* and total lack of sautéing. But the memory of my mother perfecting this dish, then carrying the aroma on her while waiting in her Vauxhall Viva to pick me up from school still lingers. This recipe sits amongst the classics too, despite its total lack of *je ne sais quoi*, it stands up for itself and is in essence a British culinary triumph, cocked at the bad divorce that is France and England.

Cut 1kg of braising steak into smallish cubes and place in a large oven-proof dish. Slice two large onions and add to the meat. Pour over enough water to just cover, season with salt and pepper and a bay leaf, cover with foil and place in an oven at 180°C for 1½ hours. Remove from the oven, cool and place it in the fridge for a day or two. Reheat the dish in an oven at 200°C / 400°C / Gas 6 for 30 minutes. Add Bisto or a paste of flour and gravy browning to thicken the sauce

Serve with freshly steamed broccoli and mashed potato. The genius of this dish is the backwards marinating and the accompanying vegetables cooked to perfection. My mum would cook the veg to death but, considering that they are the only part of this dish that I would eat, I'm a bit of a stickler for al dente.

4. Tea with Ginger

December 1981

Jo moved into the top floor flat of the student house just after Christmas. She was a fellow art student whose lightning sarcasm, sharp style and worldly ways had initially unsettled me. Jo was from Liverpool. She didn't make chit chat. She made very funny, astute and pointed remarks about all the things that got in her way. She hated Cheltenham and all the upper class twits who lived there; the ridiculousness of the 'ruling classes', who seemed to think that your old school was a really good thing to mention when you were a grown-up. We became inseparable outsiders and battled together against the establishment. We read her dictionary of quotations by candlelight, and felt the warm glow of our enduring friendship settle around us like a warm blanket.

'I grow old, I grow old, I wear my trousers rolled,' spluttered Jo, as hot tea sprayed from her mouth. 'Come on Alice, put your boring friggin' project away and let's study this book.'

I discarded my half-hearted designs and leapt onto the sagging sofa. Within minutes we were sailing away to a sepia land, with a crackly recording of Edith Sitwell replaying endlessly on the turntable in Jo's untidy room.

We got drunk at parties and liked to dance like whirling dervishes. Jo danced very well, her dark hair (coloured all shades of red, ginger and orange) streaming behind her like a time lapse photograph. She was heavily into the Liverpool scene. She took me there once and I began to clearly see why all the pompous, lazy and landed ones of the soft south of England were beyond her comprehension. The grit, talent and wit of the young people of decaying Liverpool could smash away the spoilt southerners in an instant, if only they had the chance.

Her own humour and artistic talent were outstanding, but frequent bouts of amazing sloth tended to extinguish the flow at crucial moments. In between our brilliant to downright sickly competitiveness at college, we were bonded by our dressingup antics. We'd photograph each other doing outlandish things in bizarre settings and thoroughly enjoyed shocking people. Sometimes it felt as if we were two half drowned women finding a bit of companionship and safety in our tallmasted student house. Our dark humour and irreverence was splendid and brave, but looking back I can see neither of us could have guessed what dark things lay waiting for us in the shallows.

Our fancy dress antics were inspired. We dressed as young homosexual men, with tight ripped jeans and huge bulges made from socks stuck down the front. Sported sets of keys, beard stubble shaded on our peachy skin and dark eyebrows nearly meeting in the middle. At other events we would turn up as old ladies clutching Queen Elizabeth-style 1950s handbags. Short curled grey wigs on our heads, hand-knitted cardigans, bifocal glasses, thick American tan tights and bowling shoes.

It was the extent and quality of the jumble sales in posh Cheltenham at that time that made our wardrobes so versatile. Cheltenham was favoured as a final watering hole for the Raj and returning displaced aristocrats and civil servants from the dead Empire. Perhaps the allure was its steamy microclimate at the foot of the Cotswold escarpment, and the town's veneer of genteel manners and exquisite buildings hiding its blowsy Regency past. But at any rate, their exotic legacy was our bounty. We bypassed stuffed elephant footstools and headed for hatboxes, steamer trunks and the battered hand luggage of a golden age. The most prized sported tattered boarding tickets and printed glimpses of hotels in Biarritz, Baden Baden and Singapore. Men's dress jackets, military dress jackets, bias cut gowns by *Vionnet*, plumed hats and voluminous white nightgowns made from cotton that my ancestors in Lancashire must have spun as children. We pushed Tesco shopping trolleys laden with history, adventure, allure and bereavement down wet autumnal roads at twilight. Yet, despite all the grand historical characters we could have played, Jo's favourite guise was elfin and mine was alien.

There isn't much of a recipe to pass on from this era. Food wasn't on the table; it got in the way of the drinking. One thing that Jo and I did enjoy enormously was a nice pot of tea after a hard day of being eccentric. This recipe entered my repertoire after we frequented a sweet little tea shop in Cheltenham. Their version was too weak and we had to smuggle in our own shortbread biscuits to keep costs down. The owner was so nice though. He always kept a straight face when we came in dressed as old ladies.

Recipe for Tea with Ginger

Warm a teapot with freshly boiled water, made from water from the cold tap. The old adage goes one for you, one for me and one for the pot, but that must have come from a 1940s tea rationing campaign. I tend to whack in about two dessertspoonfuls of loose-leaf Ceylon tea. Peel and finely slice a 5cm chunk of fresh ginger. Refill with boiling water and let it brew for 8 minutes with the tea and ginger. I like it with a dash of milk first and then the tea, topping it up with fresh tea at regular intervals. I never strain the tea leaves, as it's pleasant to imagine that you can read things into them.

5. Spinach Walnut and Olive Oil

July 1982

Three young women; one brunette and two blondes. Our nicknames Spinach, Walnut and Olive Oil. The white cliffs of Dover receded, and we moved to the prow of the ferry to face whatever the continent had to teach us. We felt we were well-equipped, what with backpacks, naivety, and train passes for unlimited student travel in Europe for a month. Our ultimate destination was Africa, mainly because Morocco was the furthest our money would take us and the mere mention of it aroused immediate protests from our parents. I did have some issues with travelling with one sexy blonde (Spinach) and a self-absorbed drama student (Walnut), we were all eighteen years old and ripe for life. I was Olive Oil; dark haired and terribly sensitive, but hopeful that I could be strong and quick thinking when faced with danger. Ahead of us I saw time for the unveiling of hidden survival talents; skills that only surface in wars, revolutions and student vacations.

I wept like a baby on the first bus from our hometown. My mum and dad fading to small specks at the end of a street of half-timbered houses, and Walnut laughing fondly at me for being such a softy.

But the desire to break free of our small country town, and enough pocket money jangling in our shorts pockets to do it with, was reason enough for us to roll the dice. In 1982 war was in the air. While our ferry left for Boulogne, the QE2, hastily converted into a troopship, was ploughing her way out of Portsmouth harbour, and heading for the Falkland Islands.

Spain. It was fiesta time in Murcia. The record tomato harvest had prompted the biggest party of the year. Tonight, agricultural workers from the whole province flocked to the bunting-decked town square. Their work-worn clothes swapped for crisply ironed shirts and their very brightest festive attire. We caught a small branch line from Tarragona, and swung down onto the dusty station platform with our loaded rucksacks.

We were off the beaten track, in search of loud music, fireworks, sangria and local colour. We danced, we laughed, we stuck to ourselves, we watched, waited and we pretended that we were having a good time. There were no vacant hostel rooms in the cold heart of the town. No warm smiles from the old people, and no option but for us to return to the train station to spend the rest of the night propped by our rucksacks, feeling far from home.

The station was empty, except for three old black-clad couples huddled in corners dozing on each other's tired shoulders. The girls and I piled our rucksacks together and leaned against one another in the middle of the cool stone floor. Walnut suggested we sing some Beatles songs to keep our spirits up. Wary, I had it in mind that I wouldn't sleep anyway, and swallowed a couple of pep pills to keep me vigilant through the night. Spinach got some bread out of her bag, and found comfort in the stale sweetness, and in writing some bemused entry to her diary. The station clock shuddered its way to 2:00 am; my friends' singing grew drowsy and quieter. From the distance we heard shouting. Thirty very drunk young men arrived in the terminal. This was not good.

They pawed the ground and a few braver boys made loud jokes, cupping their genitals and braying like donkeys. They seemed silly and harmless, nothing that a little studied disinterest wouldn't fix. One of the old crones who had been in the station for a long time, hobbled over to the boys, I hoped to tell them to be quiet or she would call their mothers. But no, she told them something that made them clench their fists and beat the air. Said things that made their drunken eyeballs bulge and their thick necks swell. The word spread. Within a few minutes muted conversations around the hall united into a low hum, then a low pulse-like chanting began:

Malvinas, Malvinas, Malvinas.

'Oh shit!' Squeaked Spinach. 'The Falkland islands.'

To them, we personified the UK's dubious military actions against the Argentinean Junta. We were about to be punished for being British, female and unprotected.

A few of the braver youths stepped forward and began to circle our bodies huddled on the floor. No more conversations between them, just the same demonic chant: *Malvinas, Malvinas.* As more boys joined their cries.

We were stranded on the floor, unable to break out of the circle. One man hawked and spat. Others copied him. Soon their bitter and drunk peasant bile rained down on all that Margaret Thatcher stood for.

Malvinass! Sink the Belgrano! Bash the Argies! The gutter press of Britain favoured the same rhetoric as these simple people screamed that drunken night. Hysteria stirred the cannon-fodder into answering the bugle call, fostering the notion that another nation's young people should die.

We needed help. Walnut rocked and sobbed. Spinach hid her head from the spit and debris and thought of her room at home. We needed help, and I cried out to the universe,

'Dad!'

He didn't come. But another father, who worked for the railway, came into the hall. He assessed the gravity of the situation. Without hesitation he strode over to us. Shouted at the slack-mouthed youths, silenced the hissing old women, and escorted us to the immobile train on the platform. He unlocked a carriage, gave us water and locked us in again to wait for the dawn.

My two sweet friends slept in my arms. At 4:30 am the carriage was opened for all the other travellers. In swarmed the more sober boys. I watched their reflections in the glass partition opposite us, as one of them pulled his pants down and began to stroke himself. I woke the girls and we moved to the front of the train. We staggered off at the first stop.

The soft dawn light calmed us like milk. We crossed the railway lines towards a town that smelt of shit, stumbling over a dead cat on our way to an early opening café. The strong smell of cheap cigarettes and the gurgle of an espresso machine greeted us in the neon light of a new day.

We survived, wiser to the world around us. Walnut had family friends who lived in Spain. We travelled wearily to them, and were treated with kindness and care. In the jasmine perfumed garden of their beautiful villa grew a walnut tree. I helped to gather the fallen nuts with the elderly friend, and together we shelled and crushed them with sharp blows of a hammer. I will never forget the salad she served us that evening on their terrace overlooking the Mediterranean. The dish was a wondrous blend of complexity, goodness and simplicity. Life was hard, but insight and reward littered the journey like pebbles on the beach. The pungent garlic-infused dressing cleared my mind and I felt only strength and well-being.

Recipe for Salad of Spinach, Walnut and Olive Oil

Take about 500g of fresh young spinach leaves. Wash and discard any dodgy bits, soil and coarse stalks. Drain in a colander and then dry on a clean tea towel. Shred the leaves finely using a sharp knife, and place in your most beautiful salad dish. Take about 200g of shelled walnuts, place them in a plastic bag and smash them with a rolling pin until they are finely crushed. Tip the nuts onto the shredded spinach. Crush three fat cloves of garlic and mix into the salad. Add a teaspoon of sea salt, a small dash of balsamic vinegar and a very generous double glug of olive oil. Toss the salad with your hands to incorporate all the ingredients, and taste a bit to check the all important balance. If it is too bitter, then soften it with oil. Too bland, then sharpen it with vinegar. Only experience can teach you to trust your own judgment, alas.

6. Mummy Chicken

August 1984

There was a reasonable amount of studying going on in between the travelling, but as the great Danish witer, H.C. Andersen so rightly observed, *At rejse er at leve* (to travel is to live). It's always good to remember that bit about staying alive, especially when in Morocco.

I recall tentatively the time that two friends and I made our way to Marrakesh. It had become more of an ordeal than a vacation, as we stumbled into a very different culture with bare legs. On our last evening in Spain, as we sat by a warm harbour wall in Algeciras, an old man with kind eyes asked us where we were heading. When we told him Tangiers and Marrakesh: he shook his head and firmly recommended us not to go. So we went. Within two hours of arriving in Tangiers we had a knife pulled on us, were robbed and had consequently found ourselves a local guide. We hid any remaining money, and then got stoned in the souk for the rest of the afternoon. We were quick learners!

Despite initial setbacks, we soon became more streetwise and fell headlong into every situation that took our fancy. We courted danger like moths around a flame. Always scraping by and enjoying the adrenalin rush of success, as we escaped the fire once more. On our journeys of discovery we stumbled hungrily upon Moroccan cuisine, a surprise and an oasis of succulent balances of flavour. Using hand-carved spoons, we feasted on lentil soup served in brightly glazed bowls for breakfast. Tagines of steaming couscous and spiced fish, seasoned with fresh coriander and lemon. We drank sweet mint tea poured from a dizzying height into gold embossed glasses, and we nibbled like lotus eaters on street food of dried apricots, pistachios, fresh figs and unleavened bread.

We wandered the endless souks in a time-travelling sensual dream that took us back five hundred years; pyramids of spices, the pungent perfume of clove, cinnamon, musk, cumin, coriander and the base note of rotting oranges. Overwhelmed, we cast our eyes upwards and away from the intense scene, to glimpse bright flags of fluttering cloths, hanks of yarn and caged birds lamenting all that they once known to distant flashes of blue sky. Our senses aroused, we craved to experience more of the feast, but found we were always on our guard against many horny Moroccan men. Out of necessity, and pleasure, we had adopted the local costumes of brightly coloured kaftans and baggy pants. But sexual threat hung over us like a neon sign regardless of what we wore. The sign read, *Western whores and virgins. Feel free to rob, bugger and abuse.* We were getting weary of fighting for our honour.

At the back of Marrakesh the Atlas Mountains stand high, formidable and noble. We could see them when we sat on the roof of our charming little guest house, after a balanced day of being both enthralled and mobbed. We felt a little defeated and depressed, and sought some relief from the hardened city folk and hassling guides. I wondered if the distant mountains could teach us a little more about the traditional way of life, and a gentler way of being.

The next day dawned pink and perfect. We hopped into a huge yellow taxi to cruise three hours to a weekly market in a Berber village. The journey filled us with glee. Our car windows rolled down, we leaned out feeling the warm, smiling breeze and the rush of the clear air past our pricked ears. In the distance we spied a tiny moped that left its besmirching trail of cheap petrol fumes. Drawing closer we saw that the driver was wearing a pale brown *burnous* (homespun kaftan) with a high pointed hat. The costume was in itself fabulous, and was monstrously accessorized by two severed donkey thighs straddling the seat behind him. The donkey thighs were the same shade as his clothes. Once we were close enough behind him the silhouette was startling, the fat-legged sorcerer of Marrakesh. We passed him and made the taxi driver toot his horn many times. The poor man on the moped didn't share our joke; he just had lunch on his mind.

The taxi began to climb and nose its way up the torturously twisting road. The flat plain with its scatterings of irrigated lushness receded. In its place came mineralrich rocks, stunted trees and pungent wiry shrubs. We passed small towns where hoards of small children and mangy dogs chased our dusty car, squealing with delight when we waved back exuberantly. Otherwise, abandoned villages stood dry and silent, the mud bricks that they were made from simply melting back into the land. Eventually, we reached our market town destination. The nice taxi driver told us to return to the cab in two hours. These were to be two very intense hours for me in the clear mountain air.

Marrakesh had given me a feeling of vertigo, of falling through my comfort zone, space and time. This bustling market scene similar to a 14th century Flemish painting, but set in vivid sunlight with the locals in kaftans. It was delightfully domestic and self-absorbed street theatre, with no time and certainly no inclination to trouble the three maiden travellers, unlike the dissipated city dwellers had. Here life was hard and subtle manners were vital in the functioning of the little community. It was such a relief to find this treasure blossoming on rocky soil.

We wandered through the tented city of food. We gasped and laughed at the huge corral of donkeys and mules that resembled a car park. At the stalls of copper pans and teapots watched over by blue-eyed Berber tribesmen, complete with gleaming scabbards and garlands of live ammunition. The local dentist had even set-up shop on a shaded table. The tools of his trade, pliers, were proudly displayed amid a table-top strewn with fine examples of extracted teeth. The next section housed the fruit sellers with mountains of freshly-picked produce in woven baskets. Then the vegetables, eggs, breads, knives, olives and soothsayers singing their toothless slogans into the wonderful, stinking and bleating cacophony.

More animals greeted us as we made the last round of the market. We had arrived at the meat department, close to the outskirts and the tannery pits. I wandered through this area with as much open-minded curiosity as the others, but I had the seed of doubt over continuing to eat meat. My parents felt that it was just another art college fad or affectation, but for me it had always been a moral dilemma between having the ability to kill, and not just desire to eat meat. In a supermarket in my hometown I'd been sickened by tasty photographs of cuts of meat, all red, bleeding, dead and cellophane wrapped. Trips to the livestock market in Hereford had saddened me deeply, where I gazed at the soft-eyed calves all ticketed and ready for their final journey to the abattoir. Life seemed too precious; I didn't need to eat babies.

There were numerous pens filled with goats, sheep and chickens at the Moroccan market. My friends patted the frightened animals and dawdled in the intense midday heat. A deal was being struck by some men, accompanied by much hand slapping and spitting. Everything began to move rapidly. The animals' frantic bleating, strong arms subduing a small kicking goat, knife blade flashing in the sunlight, plastic bucket proffered and a river of gushing blood. Goat suspended on a wooden frame, abdomen slashed and jewel-like entrails falling silkily into a plastic baby bath.

It was all so quick, involved and dramatic. I was shocked, but my second reaction was that this was the way to approach eating meat. I simply lacked the courage to kill my own supper, so I would rather do without it.

Recipe for Mummy Chicken

Ironically, my family loves a bit of meat and find me rather cranky with my personal philosophy of eating what you have the courage to kill. I make the following recipe for them, which they love but I personally think they're silly. It's a bad title for the recipe too, but that's what my kids call this dish. So I am trapped with a house full of carnivores, being a hypocrite and they've even named the dish after me! Ah well, there's a good story that nestles neatly in its mundane feathers. And as I dutifully cleaver the meat and rub the marinade up the 'parsons nose' I know that my recipe is spicy, exotic, sophisticated and gets better as it relaxes and marinates with time. I am mummy chicken.

Firstly, assemble the marinade. Simply place all the ingredients directly into a liquidiser or food processor and blitz to a smooth paste. It's a heady mix that takes in a tour around the Kasbah, without the hassle. Here are my suggestions for the spice mix but you can use what is at hand and improvise to your heart's content:

Roughly chop an onion, measure 3 teaspoons of coriander seeds, 3 teaspoons of cumin seeds, 1 teaspoon of peppercorns, 2 teaspoons of ground cinnamon, 4 whole cardamom pods, 1 red chilli, the juice of 2 whole lemons (keep the lemons after squeezing), 200ml of sunflower oil, 1 tablespoon of tomato puree and 2 teaspoons of sea salt, 8 peeled garlic cloves and a 10cm piece of peeled fresh ginger. Blend it all until it becomes smooth, pungent and mysterious.

Take about 1000g of chicken. I prefer to chop a chicken into portions with a glinting cleaver. Pour the marinade all over and massage it into the meat. Slice the discarded lemons into lengthways segments, squeeze and work into the mixture. Finally, take 2 teaspoons of cumin seeds, 2 teaspoons of nigella (black cumin) seeds and 4 bay leaves and scatter over the chicken. Mix all the ingredients thoroughly together with your hands again, squeezing the lemons and knowing that the acid tenderises the meat.

Cover and leave to marinate in the fridge for a minimum of four hours, but three days is much better. To cook, set your oven at 200°C / 400°F / Gas 6. Place the marinated chicken into an ovenproof dish and roast for 80 minutes, remembering to turn the sizzling chicken over once. Garnish with a generous flurry of chopped fresh coriander or parsley.

Serve with The Great Australian Bite salad, *tzatziki,* flatbreads or *naan*. The chicken is tender, aromatic and wonderful eaten hot or cold.

7. Designer Birthday Cake

November 1990

Chelsea days and South London nights. Art college led me to London town, where the streets are paved in gold to seek fame and fortune. I easily became part of the illusion, as the red bus lurched and plied the route from the mean streets south of the rive to plump South Kensington. I watched the wealth unfold from the top deck, looking probably more like I belonged to the destination but with a weekly income that didn't quite match my aspirations. I lived in Streatham, in a large rented apartment on the top floor of a Victorian mansion. I'd painted the walls and polished the floors, tiled the bathroom and had the landlord eating out of my hand as he beheld the transformation. I'd made a nice home, again, in Mount Ephraim Road. Which I was happy to discover alluded to a place of growth - a wooded, fertile environment.

To pay for my apartment I worked as a decorator in a huge design emporium in Chelsea. I'd only been there for a month, but was finding my niche and having an active time working in a team of four young creative people. There was just one other female; a blessedly straightforward, clever and happy girl called Tina. I liked her very much and decided that we'd be firm friends. At the end of the second month it was Tina's twentieth-second birthday, which I arranged to celebrate by bringing something sweet to share with a few others.

Balancing some profiteroles in a box on the top floor of the bus, with a couple of bottles of decent cava chilling in the fridge at work and decorations in my rucksack I felt rather pleased with myself. It was approaching Guy Fawkes Night, the 5th of November when the usually tolerant citizens of Great Britain torch effigies of Elizabethan Catholics and celebrate them being hung, disembowelled and chopped-up. Luckily it's about fireworks too, and I'd easily found some dinky little sparklers to adorn Tina's treat with and show my new colleagues a thing or two about events and decoration!

The reception was planned for eleven o'clock, and when all was prepared in the basement workshop I went to the office and asked a secretary to pause the piped jazz music and make an announcement over the tannoy,

'Tina Wyatt, could Tina Wyatt please go to the display office immediately.'

That was the code word for a handful of her new friends to gather and cry,

'Surprise!' and launch into, 'Happy Birthday to you…'

Six people excitedly assembled in the tiny studio, the seventh was on look-out and rushed back in squealing,

'She's coming, quick light the sparklers!'

The cava corks popped and I struggled to effectively light all the sparklers at the same time. It was impressive; the fireworks happily raged awaiting the birthday girl. At that moment Tina pushed open the door and was met by a huge pall of acrid smoke and the horrified faces of the party revellers. I hopelessly proffered the offending dessert, as another guest mouthed,

'Oh shit, the fire alarms!'

The design emporium consisted of more than just 1000 m2 of modernist retail space, packed with design classics by the metre for discerning professionals. Within its minimalist walls you could find *Charles Eames* chaise longues, *Phillipe Stark* dining tables, soft four-poster beds with Irish linen sheets, *Kenzo* cutlery and just about every other designer need catered to from the cradle to the grave. It also housed two restaurants on the first and second floors and a large publishing house on the third. The fire alarms were well-designed too, and sounded on all four floors. From the smoke-filled basement I heard the symphonic relay of bells and hooters, and with wide-eyes observed the flashing red lights and petrified stampede of my normally cool and trendy colleagues.

Standing very alone in the dispersing smoke, the party-goers having scarpered at top speed for fear of being implicated in my gunpowder plot, I weighed-up the options:

1. Run home to mother and resume my dream to become a Jack Russell dog.
2. Run and hide in a designer cupboard.
3. Shit myself.
4. Face the music.

In a flash I decided to own up and stop the chain reaction. Walking against the wave of panicked young faces, and pushing the door of the managing director's office I walked in, finding him reaching for his coat and already wearing a pained look on his face.

'You'd better get out of here, Miss Bonneville!' he barked over the cacophony of bells and abandon ship sounds. 'There's a bloody emergency on you know.'

'I know, I know. I did it,' I said, with my head down.

He didn't hear me, and continued reaching for his scarf, heading for the door and pulling me along.

'No, wait! I lit sparklers in the display office, all the smoke, lots of smoke. Sorry, I'm so sorry.'

He slowly registered my excruciating confession, staring angrily into my unnaturally pale face for the first time and registering that I'd taken full responsibility. He stood still and slowly said,

'Sparklers?'

'Yes, sparklers in Tina's birthday cake and I didn't think about the smoke or the smoke alarms or the water sprinklers.' I sadly groaned.

'Water sprinklers! Are the water sprinklers on?' he screamed.

'What about the *Noguchi* coffee tables and the £60,000 that we'll lose in takings this morning?' He seethed.

'And the *Arne Jacobsen* Egg chair that Dustin Hoffman is coming to sit in and the…'

Then seeing me go paler still, he stopped ranting. Gallantly taking off his cashmere overcoat and, placing it over my shoulders, ushered me up the emergency stairs and pushed open a fire door.

'Hurray!' cheered a sea of faces on the pavement as the door banged open and smashed into a wall with a flourish. The word had got round about the new girl and the birthday cake with firework decorations.

'What an idiot!' they all laughingly agreed, but the chefs from the Michelin starred restaurant looked fearsome, with their soufflés collapsed and the glint of *Sabatier* filleting knives in their eyes. The suited publishers frowned as their almost clinched deals lay in shreds, and the crumpled authors beamed at all the new material this unlikely incident produced. Dustin Hoffman smiled appreciatively at the street theatre, crossed his arms and took a ringside seat on a parking cone.

I felt all eyes upon me, and staggered a little in the fond golden glow of memorably interrupting the monotony of a normal working morning. With the expensive cashmere coat clinging attractively on my shoulders, and the touch of the managing director still on my arm I felt extremely embarrassed, but very grateful that she wasn't stashed in a cupboard or driving at top speed to the Welsh borders.

Relaxing a little in the glow of her newly found friends coming to embrace me, the distant sirens of two Borough of Chelsea and Kensington fire engines tore loudly around the corner of Fulham Road and Sloane Avenue and squealed to a halt in front of me.

For the rest of that day I hid up a ladder making top displays of wooden utensils and knives in the kitchen department. I felt mortified and rather worried about the unknown victims of chip pan fires, who'd never managed to get the fire fighters to arrive in time. Now was the time to hide in a cupboard, wait for my career in interior design to be effectively extinguished and seize the opportunity to become a Jack Russell. But there was a glimmer of hope as:

- I'd owned up in the nick of time.
- The sprinkler system was faulty and hadn't gone off.

The managing director fiercely rapped the bottom of the stepladder half an hour later.

'Ms. Bonneville, can you come down this instant!' he barked two metres below me.

Bottom first, I descended the ladder and prepared myself for sentencing.

'You know you're a bloody idiot and a complete liability, and we've lost £95,000 in sales this morning?' he sternly said.

I groaned and placed my head on an *Alessi* chopping block and handed him a *Nesmuk Jahrhundertmesser* carbon steel meat cleaver.

'But,' he paused and humour sparkled in his eyes, 'You are very well brought up young lady, and I'd like to thank your parents for you being so honest and in owning up so quickly! You're still a bloody idiot though,' he thoughtfully added and went to dine out on the story for the rest of the week.

Recipe for Designer Birthday Cake

There wasn't actually a delicious homemade birthday cake travelling with me that morning on the bus, it was frozen profiteroles from Iceland - the shop, not the country. But I really did aspire to recreating the glorious *croquembouche* pyramid of profiteroles that I'd gazed at by torchlight in her weekly subscription of *Cordon Bleu* Cookery magazine as a child. This recipe isn't for the faint-hearted, and first of all make sure that you have plenty of time and energy to pour into it. I had to wait for thirty years to make it properly in my kitchen in Denmark - but it was well worth the wait!

Preheat oven to 200°C / 400°F / Gas 6. Line 3 large baking sheets with greaseproof paper. Sift 150g of plain cake flour into a large bowl and have a (designer) wooden spoon at the ready. Put 300ml of just boiled water on high heat in a saucepan and add 125g of butter. Cover with a lid and bring to the boil. As soon as the mix is boiling vigorously, take off the heat. Remove lid and quickly add the flour in one go. Beat vigorously with the wooden spoon until glossy and mixture comes away cleanly from the sides of the pan in one smooth ball. Spoon into the empty flour bowl and set aside to cool completely. Gradually beat two eggs into the cooled flour mixture until smooth and glossy. Spoon into a large piping bag fitted with a 1 cm plain nozzle. Pipe 4 cm wide x 3 cm high mounds onto the prepared baking sheets, spacing them about 3 cm apart. Use a damp finger to flatten any peaks. Bake for 20-25 minutes until puffed and golden. Remove from the oven and, once cool enough to handle, pierce the base of each bun with a skewer to allow steam to escape. Return to oven, hole side up for 3 minutes. Cool completely on a wire rack.

At this point you might be wishing that you had bought some frozen ones, or made a trip to Iceland! But these profiteroles are extraordinary, so grab a strong macchiato in a *Georg Jensen* cup and persevere.

For the vanilla cream, whip 800 ml of double cream and 4 tbsp of icing sugar in a large bowl until they resemble soft peaks. Cut and scrape the seeds out of a vanilla pod and add to the mixture. Spoon half of the mixture into a piping bag with a 1 cm plain nozzle. Pipe cream into the buns (make skewer holes a little bigger first) until full but not bursting. Re-fill the piping bag as needed and store the filled buns in the fridge until you're ready to assemble the masterpiece.

We're talking design here, and I was (am) a girl who generally 'went too far,' so why stop here? So I've added chocolate-dipped strawberries to adorn and amaze.

Melt both 40g of dark (70% minimum) chocolate and 15g of white chocolate in separate bowls set over pans of barely simmering water. Dip the bottom half of 10 perfect strawberries into dark chocolate and put on a wire rack set over a baking sheet to collect drips. Drizzle over a little melted white chocolate and leave to set in a cool place.

When you are ready to assemble the croquembouche, put a large, flat cake stand into the fridge to chill while you make the chocolate 'glue'. Melt 175g of dark chocolate in a bowl set over a pan of barely simmering water, then sift in 2 tbsp of icing sugar and stir until smooth. Turn off the heat under the pan, but keep the bowl set over the water while you put all your hard work together. Remove the cake stand from the fridge. Place a small 16cm bowl upside down on the plate, using about 12 profiteroles, dip the bases into the chocolate 'glue' and position on the cake stand to make a circle (make sure the profiteroles sit snugly together). Dip remaining profiteroles one by one in chocolate, then put them on top of this base layer, arranging them in a conical tower. Place another 11cm bowl on top of the larger one and keep layering the profiteroles to the very top.

This designer palaver is nearly over and all that remains is to make a chocolate sauce by heating 100g of dark chocolate, 150g of double cream and 2 tbsp of golden syrup in a bowl set over a pan of simmering water until melted. Remove from the heat and stir until smooth.

Pour into a serving jug and set aside to cool for 10 minutes before drizzling over the profiterole tower and serving with the dipped strawberries around the base of the plate and sparklers stuck all over the cake.

P.S. Serve outside!

8. French Dressing

August 1992

Paris, the city where you find couples snogging by every bridge. Fine limestone dust coating your shoes as you wander through the Jardin des Tuileries, and small rolls of old carpet diverting the street-washing water down culverts in the sidewalk. I stood gazing out of the window of my small apartment on the Quai des Grands Augustins breathing in my luck, and exhaling the rancid air from the busy road below. To my right were the Notre Dame and the Pont St Michel. Before me, the Seine slid past the Palais de Justice. I was 29 years old, it was a hot summer evening and my life was unfolding beautifully in front of me.

That Sunday had been spent sitting by the river wielding my needle-nosed pliers at a coil of steel wire. Small sculptures of fishes appeared. Fantastical creatures that could never swim in the Seine swam with pleasure from a part of my imagination overflowing with glee. They arrived at my fingertips also as a foil to confuse men. Although French men were renowned sexual predators, the sight of an attractive woman doing something weird with pliers did seem to suggest that I was not quick shag material. Generally French men seemed as if they always dressed in the same beige raincoats and fiddled in their pockets. (All while undressing you with their dark eyes and licking their painful, stubble-encased lips.)

I'd seized the chance to relocate with the interior design company. My London life had been neatly packed into two battered trunks, that I'd found when I was a student. They were shipped across the Channel to chaperone me and to rekindle their past adventures.

My first Sunday in Paris, just five months earlier, was spent exploring the Jardin du Luxembourg. I'd sat in a sunny place with a contented sigh, a book to read and an apple to eat, marvelling at my arrival accompanied by sparrows celebrating the first day of spring. Immaculate children with knickerbockers and velvet-collared coats sailed toy yachts in the large ornamental lake. Three pages into the book a shadow crossed the page:

'*C'est un livre passionnant?*' I looked up in shock. A tall and darkly shaven man with brown eyes, a foppish oiled hairstyle, hairy knuckles and THAT raincoat gazed down at my book and licked his bruise-coloured lips.

'*Mais non, monsieur.*' I squeaked, as a blush and the hot breath of casual continental carnality swept my way. 'Bugger off and leave me alone, *allez allez!*' I added for maximum impact. Indignant fury rising and my crap French firing on all cylinders.

A look of confusion and disbelief crossed his face: was I seriously rejecting his offer of a quick and energetic bout of giggi giggi in a hotel room with carpet on the walls? Then THAT raincoat disappeared into the well groomed undergrowth. In search of his wife and immaculate children no doubt. I felt flustered and hunted. I moved on to another part of the gardens, in search of my long dreamed of seclusion and success at having escaped from hard and grimy London. I found a well-positioned chair, ripped my way through the apple, polished my sunglasses and concealed any sexually suggestive and visible body parts. Retrieving the novel from my pocket, I settled back into my new life in France with a contented sigh.

Eight pages later:

'C'est une livre passionnel?'

Unbelievable! I was too angry to look up. THAT raincoat had courage. A long minute passed until I finally looked up at yet another middle-aged and horny man. This time he had donkey-brown corduroy trousers, a huge nose, round glasses and a moustache that looked like it was pasted on. I had to laugh at the poor man urgently fondling his pecker and looking like Groucho Marx. He disappointedly hobbled away.

The use of sharp pointed tungsten-tipped pliers to clip, bend and cajole steel wire into intricate shapes was not accidental. As I sat on my cushion on the sunny, peed-on embankment of the Seine, no horny Frenchman dared to come close to me and my worrying pastime. Little fish sculptures poured from my singing snips into a black velvet pouch. They would be glazed with bright silk paper and suspended as mobiles and earrings in the privacy of my high-ceilinged seventeenth century apartment. My home measured just 35 square metres. I'd painted the walls a deep burnt orange; all the furniture that I'd found in local skips, a peppy gecko green. My bed was two purple-covered mattresses that doubled-up in daytime as seating with squashy patterned cushions. From this tiny womb like environment, I managed to cook and drink most French and international friends under the table. The music invariably veered towards the 1920s: Bix Beiderbecke, Edith Piaf or Josephine Baker. My hair bobbed and hennaed and my clothing sleek, startling and shiny. Large hats, tall flat boots, vampire red lips and *Guerlain* perfume. My mum egged me on and bought me a long ebony cigarette holder; I stole a silver cigarette case from a man with lecherous intentions and took to smoking *Gitanes*...That was until the day my feisty French friend Claudette said,

'Alice, why are you smoking these stinking shits? It is the big, hairy *camion* drivers who are preferring them.'

To me they were the essence of France when I arrived in Dieppe, en route for a family holiday in the 1970s. In retrospect, I guess that there were plenty of truck drivers around at the time.

I was so in love with Paris. I fell for the city like a foolish man with a beautiful courtesan. She dazzled me on a daily basis. I slavishly drooled in every courtyard of the innumerable hôtel particuliers that peppered my stomping grounds of the fifth, sixth and seventh arrondissements. I wept for joy in the street markets filled with squeezable vegetables, furry mould or leaf-covered cheeses, brighteyed fish and crustaceans brought from the coast that morning, and the babble of the throng ministering to the French compulsive disorder that is gastronomy. Equipped with a large basket and straw hat, I was overwhelmed as I paced the mediaeval incline of the Rue Mouffetard hunting for the dish of the day.

That evening in the Quai des Grands Augustins I began to open my windows to the hot noise of the street and the river. The sightseeing boats had begun their evening floodlit patrol of the sights of Paris, armed with lasers and giving tourists the time of their lives. I was fresh from the shower and perfumed with vetiver soap, glowing from a day in the sun and wearing a cream silk kaftan and no knickers. As I pulled the old windows open, a hot breeze rushed at me and blew up my loose kaftan and between my legs. I gasped and lay on my cushion-strewn mattress laughing, as the little suspended fishes twirled in endless spirals in the orange air, the silhouetted balcony rail rotated around my pretty home and the *Bateau Mouche* sailed by.

Recipe for French Dressing

Take a clean, resealable glass bottle (an empty 500ml olive oil bottle is perfect). Pour in 1/3 balsamic or white wine vinegar. Add 2/3 good olive oil, 2tsp sea salt, plenty of ground black pepper, about 5 crushed cloves of garlic, 4tsp Dijon mustard, 3 whole bay leaves, plenty of chopped French tarragon or thyme. Simply screw the top on the bottle, shake it well and then use. I tend to keep mine going in the fridge for a couple of weeks. It marinates and improves with time. Take it out of the fridge 30 minutes before you need to use it so the olive oil can liquefy. A real Parisian would omit the heavy use of garlic, as most of them work in office environments and so prefer not to stink like someone from the Mediterranean or recently arrived from Great Britain.

9. Gratin Dauphinois

April 1994

I made Gratin Dauphinois for dinner last night. As my nine year old daughter struggled to peel the muddy potatoes, my mind cast itself back to Jean-Paul. He was my peculiar neighbour in Paris, who introduced me to this rich and creamy concoction served in a stolen Limoges dish.

Jean-Paul was a lost soul. He first told me of his noble family from Brittany and their Chateau overlooking the Atlantic Ocean:

'On zee beach, below zee chateau, you are finding 'orses 'eads after a big storm,' he told me on the night he met me from the Gare du Nord, then drove me to his fancy apartment in the 7th *arrondissement.* I accepted his generosity and far-fetched tales with all the gratitude of one who arrives in a strange land with nothing but a suitcase and one friend in that country. Perhaps I conveniently forgot that old chestnut *There's no such thing as a free lunch*, but this handsome Frenchman, with just a hint of expensive makeup on, seemed to be a genuinely friendly person.

He gave me a perfect avocado drizzled in fruity olive oil, served on a bed of pungent and bitter salad leaves and a cut glass goblet of chilled *Pouilly Fumé*. I was impressed; I appreciated all the attention lavished on that humble avocado. He showed me the monstrous coffee table that he had made from a sheet of glass resting on cairns of granite from his beloved Brittany, slavishly flicking through the interior design books resting upon it and name dropping for a good half hour. My eyes and ears grew tired, after my journey from England by rail; the train curving out of sight from Victoria station like for all those soldiers before me, my homeland theatrically receding behind the white cliffs of Dover and rattling through the Somme on a trench foot October day. Jean-Paul saw my exhaustion, and kindly ran me a deep bath from golden taps and poured precious oils and perfumes into the swirling mist. As I lay I breathed in the luxurious warmth, I felt lucky and protected. I wasn't used to being attended to by a virtual stranger, but this fussy little man seemed to need friendship and companionship as much as I did. For once in my life I accepted these gifts graciously, and lay back like a million dollars into my brand new life.

Later, I was led to a rococo four poster bed. It smelt bad though; a mixture of aftershave and a faecal overtone. I wanted then to be in a modest room that I had paid for; I smelt complications in my new life. A rattle of keys at the front door, men's voices alternating between hushed and outraged. A knock on my door and Jean-Paul coming in looking abashed, while a small dark man muttered aggressively in the corridor.

The apartment didn't belong to Jean-Paul. It belonged to his rich occasional lover; who had come back home, to do whatever he did, with a young boy with glassy eyes. We scurried around the house like thieves, bid the angry man a hasty adieu and went in search of a cheap hotel room. I found the perfect one with a stained bidet, scuffed linoleum on the floor and stiletto shoe marks on the wall over the bed. All in all my first night in Paris had taken in two deliciously disturbing slices of La vie Parisienne. I sighed contentedly and slept deeply, but it never occurred to me until years later to wonder where Jean-Paul had passed the night.

My life in Paris had begun. From the outset, with Jean-Paul's assistance, it smacked of high jinx, deception, betrayal and endless glamour. I wandered into his web of lies like a moth unused to the brightness of day. He let me down a thousand times with his weak threads and badly woven tales. Each time I forgave him and, perversely, as with most of the numerous bad things that have happened in my life, saw it all as great research for the book that I would one day write. He helped me in a thousand ways too, but always with bizarre strings attached and a twist in the tail that would bite back just when you thought you were safe. As time passed and I became more established, Jean-Paul became like a bad servant and I his mistress; who treated him fairly, listened to his creative deceptions and, foolishly, opened doors to hard won and rewarding jobs and events. Once on the threshold his unfortunate lying, cheating and plagiarism could only get him as far as the cloakroom. Jean-Paul remained a spectator of grand things, as he chewed bitterly on the bones and golden coins that I smuggled his way. He complained about the unfairness of life and how he was too often on the receiving end of brutality. As I excused myself with a lie, I had begun to see why.

We made some wonderful journeys together, if he managed to turn up. He had a very shabby white Toyota van packed full of unusual pebbles, half eaten sandwiches and mysterious boxes containing stolen goods. On crisp Sunday mornings in early spring we would head out of the city in search of real countryside, and the chance to pick some wild flowers. One thing that we had very much in common was our country upbringings and a love of wide open places, neglected chateaux, storytelling and the cold stone aroma of neglected history. We would find picturesque ruins of mediaeval towers on the plains of Melun; my rubber soled shoes clinging gingerly to the remnants of stone spiral staircases and my hands grasping at wiry plants in the algaed walls, the tower reaching above me to the clear blue unroofed sky. We wove fanciful tales about the baron and his lady that had lived there so many spring mornings ago, always slipping back in time just a little, aided and abetted by the timely tolling of an ancient church bell or the call of a startled raven. The day would roll out ahead of us like a charmed tapestry depicting our courtly love. A call at a local farm to purchase exquisite local brie, a good bottle of burgundy from Jean-Paul's hamper accompanied by two stolen crystal glasses and a Brussels lace tablecloth. Crispy Parisian baguettes would materialise from my basket, Caravaggio would have approved of the voluptuous bunches of bloomed grapes and small wooden bowls filled with farmyard tasting salty olives and tangy cornichons. Two lonely people using each other just a little, laughing at the irony of our appearance of behaving like two mediaeval lovers posing for an interior design magazine. Beneath the veneer, my secret cursing of his compulsive lies and his huge guilt for hiding his secret homosexuality from his modest Breton family. Who, incidentally, didn't live in a castle by the sea, rather a semi-detached bungalow in a small town.

I have a faded photo of a stooping man, as he walks through a muddied field of rotting sunflower heads on a misty day. He didn't know that I had taken the picture, to me this decayed image says so much of my tragic friend. A very foolish man, but his sweet heart caked in layers of monstrous lies. One day Jean-Paul wept bitterly and told me that he was HIV positive. This was at the tail-end of our friendship, but I'd had had a craw full of his deceptions and let downs and had moved on in space and time. Somehow, as he'd cried wolf so many times before, deep down inside I didn't believe him. We parted ways a short time afterwards. Jean-Paul and I lost touch. I couldn't take any more fiction. To this day I don't know if he is alive or dead and I suspect that he is alive. My mother flippantly mentioned that I shouldn't believe that he was terminally ill until the funeral cortege went by. I looked up a bit startled that she could be so rough with her words. She quickly added that he was a sweet man and a wonder at arranging the folds in her curtains.

Recipe for Gratin Dauphinois

Heat the oven to 200°C / 400°C / Gas 6. Cut 900g peeled potatoes into thin slices, about 3mm thick. Grease a deep, preferably stolen, ceramic dish with some butter. Place a layer of potatoes on top, sprinkle with salt and pepper, a little chopped garlic and some of the 1000g grated gruyere cheese. Repeat until you are at the top layer and dot with plenty of cheese and butter. Heat 275ml whipping cream and pour into the potatoes at the side of the dish. Dot with 100g butter and bake in the oven for about 50 minutes until the top is golden brown and the potatoes tender.

Warning: this is a really rich dish. Only suitable for those who aspire to grandeur, glamour, heartburn and intrigue.

10. Burnt Rice

May 1995

The constant thud thud from an unseen building site close by. A pneumatic drill pierces the hot July air. I lie frozen in blue, as my curtain billows out and into my small room in the stale breeze. Sick with sadness and neglect, my nerves jangling as if a hang-nail had snagged on nylon. I watch as the cloth expertly moves, while the curtain hooks click to the beat. I bite hard on my knuckles and wish that it was clean fabric and with a country view, any view, behind it. The view was only of my stunted geraniums in a window box, and the dirty beige side of a house two metres away. I worried about the whole stinking tenement being a fire risk, its dry wooden staircase sneaking its way arthritically up the centre of the 200 year old structure like a fuse. My tiny home lay right at the top. No way out, there seldom is for the poor and alone. I saw us burn, and all my bedding tied together could never reach the ground.

I wasn't technically poor, more financially 'embarrassed' after spending too much money. For five days a week I would wind my way from the Avenue de Clichy to the well-heeled Rue du Bac in the 7th arrondissement of Paris. Once there I would look as one amongst the designer furniture and the steel-railed glamour of the store that

I worked in. At six o'clock the charade ended though. Like a pretty clockwork toy, I would descend to the stench of the metro at Sèvres-Babylon, ready to be shuttled back to the terminally down at heel. Sometimes, in order to not go home too early, I would get out of the train at *La Fourche* station. Years later I realised that this had been the site of the notorious *Forche* prison mentioned in Charles Dickens' *A Tale of Two Cities*. In retrospect, I can see that the whole feel of the area, even still in the 1990s, consisted of menace, poverty, deprivation and pain. Many North Africans eked out a poor living in small dusty stores. I shopped in these and in Monoprix, and found myself sharing the same taste in deodorant as broken-faced transvestites, as we scanned the shelves together searching for love, success, glamour and a cheap perfume to mask the odour of sadness.

If I try to evoke a smell for those days in my viewless room, then it would be of burnt rice wafting up the stairwell from the countless bedsits below mine. For sounds it would be the thud of the pile driver on the building site in the day, and at night the low rhythmic sobbing of the sad-eyed Algerian lady next door. I had met her a couple of times on our narrow landing, as I initially tried to find a home for the pot plants that had graced the balcony of my previous flat, the price of which, coupled with my insane travelling to London to visit a worthless German boyfriend, had placed me in financial ruin. Perhaps I was in La Forche prison, in a wing reserved for debtors? The lady next door, as I eyed her through the peephole on my door, was locked away for other reasons it appeared.

Late one night, as I lay in half-sleep, the tramp of heavy boots on flimsy stairs. Many feet, coughs and deep murmuring voices. The sound grew louder and louder and was followed by sharp knocking at the door of my neighbour. I tiptoed to my own metal door and peeped through the spy hole; seven dark-haired men in cheap shoes shuffling and extinguishing cigarettes. The woman opened her door and took in her visitors with one quick glance; a look that flickers still in a small box of horror that I carry, locked away, in my nightmares.

She backed slowly into her small room crippled with fear, and the men in shiny suits swaggered in. Within ten minutes I heard large boots being cast aside, and the sickening sound of her creaking bed rocking against my thin wall. This continued for a long time. I rang for the police but they never came.

Nobody was invited to my house as it was in hell. A handful of my closest friends passed by out of loyalty. But the combination of the dreadful tenement, my ever-shorter home-cut fringe and a haunted look about my eyes drove all but the bravest away. I would sit at the end of the table like a body with no soul. They would joke and laugh, drink and never come around again. It felt marginally better to be alone. One of the few photographs that I have of that period is one taken by automatic timer. It was a Saturday night. I had been drinking red wine, writing my tortured journal and had looked up and had caught a telling reflection of myself; ruby lipped and sad eyed, I needed to claw my way back to the light.

Recipe for Burnt Rice

Perhaps my tale hasn't whetted your appetite, but cooking, like life, does take in a vast array of ingredients, experiments, mistakes and experiences. The sweet and nutty scent of this dish sizzling to crispy perfection is hard to master, especially when a desired burnt finish is required. This is a Persian dish; traditionally the most crispy and almost blackened part is reserved for the guest of honour, which may seem strange, but the black part does taste best.

Take 4dl of basmati rice, wash it well in a small saucepan, rinse and drain in a sieve. Place the rice back in the saucepan with 6dl of boiling water and a teaspoon of sea salt. Cover and bring to the boil, simmer on low for 10 minutes until half cooked. Meanwhile, melt about 50g butter in a non-stick deep frying pan. Add the rice and dot it with another 50g of butter on top and a couple of tablespoons of water. Turn off the heat and cover with a clean tea towel, making sure that you fold in the edges and don't start a fire, especially if you live in a dismal tenement! Put the pan on a low heat for about 20 minutes. To serve, flip the whole golden and perfectly burnt cake onto a big serving plate and try and explain brightly why the burnt bits are the best to your disappointed guests.

11. Stone Ground

July 1996

The rains streamed from the pumice porous clouds every two hours. Inbetween times the sun warmed the land, you could hear her humming, trembling with growth and chlorophyll green. This land, that in the soldier ant months smoked and heat hazed, grew heady with desire.

We sat in the middle of a flower-strewn meadow. No sound, only the wind buffeting the branches of cork trees and across our ears. Two women and an older man all sat facing the sun, motionless and in harmony with the huge event being enacted around us. Unseen hands caressed and soothed our softened, sun kissed faces. The wind tousled our hair and vials of purest air spread through each of our lungs like the blossoming of a tree. I lay into the flowers, into the earth. I lay still and with an enigmatic smile brushing my lips, as the green coils and fingers stroked and nuzzled my deepest thoughts and yearnings.

Beside me sat my dad, the love of my mother's life. He studied his map and consulted a worn looking *Baedeker* guide to central Portugal. A man with whom she shared a deep and secure love which she knew she would be unable to live without, come his time to leave. She dismissed such thoughts with quick hand movements and busied herself with unpacking a picnic. Out of a brown paper bag there materialised a lunch of small bruise purple olives, a salty goat's cheese and mouth staining tannic wine. She tore herself a large chunk of substantial looking flat bread and tasted a secret country.

Dad gave up studying the book and focused on the prospect of food. He went to wake me from my commune with nature. Not immediately though, thinking that I was sleeping; he wondered at my look of tranquility. The pinched look that I had worn when I arrived on a flight from Paris had evaporated. The strictly slicked down hair had returned to its natural waves, freckles had sweetly appeared in place of the mask of makeup, and I sighed a smile that made him cough and wonder at the recipient of my daydreaming. The noise brought me abruptly back from the world of plants to see my parents gazing down, in much the same way as in one of my earliest memories; as they did when I was lying in a low lit room, and looking up into those two beloved faces offering me their dreams.

After lunch we returned to our hire car parked under an ancient cypress tree. The high rolling clouds scudded over and went on to release their bounty a few hundred kilometres away to the east, on the doorstep of the Sierra de Guadalupe.

'Half an hour and we reach the stone circle,' said the dad through peppermint crunching teeth.

The strangeness of the normality of them comforted me now as it had always done. What I had just felt in the meadow surely must have touched them too? Apparently not. Dad drove on whilst I rearranged my legs and luxuriously wondered at my state of sexual arousal.

'Stop dreaming, our Alice! It says here there's a megalithic stone circle of 150 standing stones situated two kilometres from the 349 route from Évora to Tavira,' barked dad from the front seat.

The pot-holed road twisted and wove its way gently upward. Flower meadows and cork trees gave way to briar and unkempt scrubby woodland. The sweeping vistas became crouched, as canopy like trees blended branches and the light became mottled. A sign for a historical monument pointed quietly to the right of the road. Once off the tarmac, the black mud clung in huge clods to the underside of the car and the wheels spinned and spat out glossy treacle. We persevered, with gooey embraces and the mud gurgling fatly like lazy custodians. A parking place and gloomy picnic spot designated for tourists were signposted, and directions to the monument given. No other vehicle was parked; we were out of season. We three large people began to emerge from the tiny Fiat car. Not typical English strawberry blondes with sandals and socks, but well built and strong looking with dark hair. Dad first, sporting guide book and binoculars; the possibility of spotting a hoopoe always an added bonus. Next came mum, toting the ever-present handbag with passports, airline tickets, sticky old sweets and packets of tissues. Finally I uncurled myself from the back seat of the car, armed with a camera and dark glasses.

We were at once silenced from our possible chatter by a tremendous sound of the breeze rattling the new leaves in the tree tops. The coltish shoots swayed and sashayed with their new curves and buds of green lushness. Then another melody; the frantic buzz of mating insects scratching and crackling in the air, on the ground, under the ground, in the bushes, in puddles of rainwater, in the black mud. Huge coupled dragonflies flitted overhead, beetles scrambled intently around in the decayed leaves by our feet, crickets rasped their amorous song and a queen bee careered wildly past with a worker attached and three in hot pursuit. The passionate insects and the dancing foliage ushered us into the entry of the arena.

Dark undergrowth tunnelled over us and we walked at the edges of the track to avoid the black puddles. Heads down and stunned at the orgy of insects, we soon came to an open sunlit space, with the forms of upright menhirs peppering two concentric circles. The frantic musical accompaniment that had greeted our arrival now fell silent, and the sun beat down to cast short shadows from the immense stones.

We walked amongst them like sleepwalkers. Dad began reading aloud from an archaeology book and disturbing the electric tension with his scientific facts. Mum, far the more mystical, was silent and deep in thought. She was trying to imagine the original builders of the monument and why the majority of the outer circle stones looked distinctly phallic? I was close by and was having similar thoughts.

'Mum, this is incredible, these stones are all about shagging!' I squeaked. Feeling awkward and childlike in the company of my mother. But with the distinct feeling that any English prudishness was beyond us this day. A slow connection to my other sensual experiences began to grow in my imagination.

'I know, there are about sixty huge phallic male ones in the outer circle, and here they seem interspersed with other more female, receptive shapes,' she muttered, finding it difficult to not be overwhelmed by the idea that we were the first people to ever have professed these thoughts. Her reserve was evaporated, she'd said phallic.

'It's all about fertility and sexuality isn't it,' I said. There was no need for my sexologist mother to answer.

It was an epiphany to realise the desire and urgency that seethed within the circle. The outer stones seemed to wait their turn, hard and erect for twenty thousand years. The passage of so much time was not evident on the sharply hewn boulders. No vandalism here as with so many other stone circles, be it by reusing the stones for building purposes, or by zealous priests destroying pagan images. No, these stones were intact. They spoke of arousal, of the back arching timelessness of sex and procreation, and the supremacy of nature.

'I bet that the locals have always worshipped on the sly here, it's far more appealing than that chapel in Évora,' I said after making another tour of the inner circle.

The chapel, which we had visited the day before, had been entirely decorated with 5000 human skeletons. It was a catacomb above ground called an ossuary. The bones had been laid out in intricate patterns, with baroque columns and gilded plaques from the 15th century. Femur bones on one level, all sloping to the left. Then came tibia to the right and gaping skulls in the middle. A little scattering of knuckles and hip bones, and then grandly topped off with half ribs in a conch shell like design. Ghastly, the place was rank with the pervading smell of death. The largest domed and skull encrusted ceiling had two shrunken leathery figures dangling down from its centre. A man and a tiny infant, suspended for four hundred years. No explanation, no guidebook, only the hint of the idea of the historic concern with pain. In its unquestionable power and bizarre decorative approach I imagined a palette of inventive martyrdoms, inquisitorial torture and torments of the damned. The place was all about the fear of God, the brutality of man and the power of the church. Our stone circle glowed in comparison with honesty, urgency, fun and fertility.

'Well, what does this shape represent?' asked dad, giving up on his factual book and getting swept into his womenfolk's newly developed ritual sex theory. This first stone struck me as that of a woman, ample backside pushed outwards and upwards, body arched and breasts stuck out. I gave mum the camera and said,

'Like this!'

I struck the exaggerated pose and mum photographed me alongside the stone. It would do as an explanation; we were convinced that we were anthropological detectives' hot-on-the-heels of history. Other stones on the inner circle begged for attention. A massive block with carved swirls for breasts was next.

'Can you take this one?'I called.

I hoisted up my sun top, and was photographed with bare breasts next to the huge swirling goddess. Other stones presented equally explicit interpretations. Mother made suggestions and I struck the poses. Bent double and touching my toes and thighs. The stones lacked legs, but you could always locate the buttocks, pudenda and breasts. The camera clicked and dad smiled benignly, feeling himself and the science community pleasingly overruled by his whirling women. Still, the silence of the place hovered as if holding its breath in shock. Black flies began to pester him. He swatted them and returned to watching the modern priestesses work themselves into a frenzy of possibilities.

'It must be the sacrificial slab!' l gasped.

Alone in the centre or the circle I found myself confronted with a low table like stone. I lay on it with legs apart, arms stretched out and theatrically arched my back ready for the ultimate Stone Age shag. Suddenly, the sky above me darkened dramatically, and black flies dive-bombed me and my pose off the slab and away from the moment. I had gone too far. I tried to swat them away, but only succeeded in making myself hotter and more desirable. My parents too were fighting the air wildly. The tropical chant of the insects and the breeze in the trees picked up again with the beat of the flies droning wings. Like nightclub bouncers, the black guardians escorted the startled interlopers unceremoniously out of the arena. With rough manners they pushed and slapped us along, requesting a little less pseudocarnal knowledge, and more respect in this sacred place. The bushes swayed and mysteriously parted as we fleeing desecrators disappeared up the muddy pathway. The sound of our car driving off was followed by the deafening sound of the preoccupied insects resuming the orgy.

We hastily drove another route away from the stone circle. A small gravel road was suggested on the map, it led down from the high elevation to a small settlement and eventually to another B road. We swatted the remaining black flies and made breathless attempts at dealing with the intensity of the recent unsettling situation. There was the feeling that we had stumbled into a magically charged place. That we had guessed the riddle of the stones, but had desecrated the shrine. The intensity of the experience was beyond us. Dad began to smother our experience with fact and science. Mum and I swapped notes on the incident for several years.

Silent and lost in thought, I squeezed the fabric of the upholstered seat to remind myself of the plastic reality of the end of the twentieth century. The chances to travel had grown with my new job with a French luxury brand, and luxurious hotels and restaurants around the world opened their doors to me. This time I'd been in Lisbon, where after a star-studded event my parents had come to share my triumph and had planned this much needed week away. I was struggling to cope with the hollow reality of the jet-set, and cracking into deeper and deeper fissures beneath the perfumed exterior. I welcomed the thought of another way of being, a way out of the maze that directed me through the cold and brittle heart of fashionable society. For once the close proximity of my parents kept me calm and the deep magic of this place kept me alive and aspiring.

The recent spring rains had re-carved this ancient track. A deep gully had formed to the right, so the little front wheel drive car clung bravely to the left hand side. The going was slow, but steep and thrilling. Ten minutes into the descent, the wooded heights of the circle receding, we came to a deep crevasse gouging out the track. All of us piled out of the car and discussed the options. There was only one, to go on. There was no chance of turning back and tackling the steep incline on loose shingle. After a swig of water we all helped to form a causeway of rubble and wood across the mini canyon. Once across, I scouted ahead for jagged rocks and branches that blocked the way. I thundered down the hillside clearing the route; I was strong, I was sure footed, and I felt better than I had done in years. The little Fiat Punto inched its way down the dramatic track. I found a resting place after my road building; I lay in the grass and waited.

A strong desire to sleep came across me, but I stood up again and walked back towards the direction of the car. It felt uneasy to stop moving and be alone in this empty landscape of twisted cork trees and lengthening shadows, as if I was observed by thousands of curious eyes. Within ten minutes of uncomfortable waiting, the car appeared, with my beloved parents beeping the horn and waving merrily at this sinister place. The car had performed beyond its brand expectations. Would the rental company ever know? The heavy breathing shadows retracted and slid into the ground.

We reunited and toasted our impressive civil engineering with bottled water and wide smiles. The flower-strewn meadows softened the tree lined summit from this angle. The low hum of busy insects and the hush of the wind played in the background. All was calm, yet still intent and predatory. I wandered off looking for somewhere to pee. At this point I felt observed but unconcerned, apart from my family there was not a living soul around. A straggly old cork tree offered a little cover in the open pasture. I squatted and peed long into the grass, then placed an offering of my bloodied tampon in the branches.

Recipe for Stone Ground Bread

I don't really have any Stone Age recipes to hand, but could twist history a little and offer you this great recipe for a rustic bread made from spelt flour; an ancient type of wheat favoured by early civilisations, also considerably higher in protein than our modern genetically messed around wheat flours. Spelt grains have been found in prehistoric tombs and sites in and around southern Europe right up to mediaeval times.

In a very large lidded saucepan heat 2dl milk and 1dl of live natural yoghurt to blood temperature. Remove from the heat and crumble in 25g of fresh yeast and stir. Take 250g of wholemeal spelt flour and add to the yeast mixture, then 2 teaspoons of olive oil, 3 teaspoons of sea salt and 2 teaspoons of runny honey. Stir with your hand, and then knead vigorously for about 8 minutes. Place it back in the warm saucepan and leave it to rise in a warm place for about 45 minutes. Turn the oven to 220°C / 425°F / Gas 7 and place your beautiful ancient dough in the middle of a greased baking sheet and decorate with tribal slashes. Place a clean tea towel over it and place in a warm place for about 30 minutes to rise again. Glaze with water and place high up in the really hot oven for about 30 minutes.

Serve your ancient bread still warm and savour a secret country. I like to eat huge chunks of it with stinky unpasteurised cheese, a drizzle of honey, some pungent olives and a few glasses of robust red wine shared with my mystical mother.

12. Shortbread

May 1997

A small miracle sprouted inside. Our first baby had decided upon us, and descended from her twinkling star on a clear and icy winter's night. I smoothed my lover's warm hands across my belly and smiled at our darling *Pip*, safely ensconced in her watery world and nourished with never ending love.

On clear, cold spring mornings I wrapped in warm clothes, and contentedly strolled around the mediaeval nunnery, known as the *Beguinhof*, where, in the 13th century a progressive community of nuns, single women, children and widows has once lived. Nowadays visiting academics to the University of Leuven live there, and so it too became our wonderful neighbourhood. I felt a warmth and acceptance from the old red buildings. I smiled like the Giaconda at every red brick, window casing and worn cobble. The gracious, wimple bedecked buildings noted my ability to realise the past. They nodded their consent at my glowing, yet preoccupied eyes. Then blessed me and prayed for my morals. Albeit a little loose, but as in their golden age, young women should be proven to be fertile prior to their nuptials. They all nodded in agreement, and retrieved old memories of when their own extraordinary community had thrived.

With an absent minded air, they collectively sighed and returned to their needlework.

I stopped for a while on the sunny back steps of a gothic church. I began to compose a letter to my mother, explaining her wayward daughter's newly found contentment. After four sentences my concentration was broken by high, sweet notes played on a flute inside the old church. I lifted my head and sat back in the weak sunlight, feeling it wash over me in gentle, lapping waves. This place, that I had fled to from Paris, had graced me with a new life to nurture and the wisdom of a thousand years.

One day in late spring I took a bike ride. There were clear skies, soft wisps of spun sugar clouds and the sound of scooters revving insanely in the distance. I packed water, juicy peaches and a blanket for a shady nap, and then pedalled sedately through the twisting old centre of the town, past the belching ring road and back onto quiet old roads; sunken paths, that once conveyed the cloth merchants pack horses on their way to Ghent, Mechlen and Bruges.

The hedgerows were swathed in extravagant plantings of cow parsley, forget-me-not's, mallow and briar rose. I breathed the sharp sweet perfumes in, and told Pip how she would make garlands for her and her little sister's hair on such a pretty May morning. A soft wind blew and made the tall dry grasses sway. Thousands of thistle seeds billowed into the air and parted noiselessly as the bicycle clicked and ratcheted through them at a steady pace.

After leaving the outskirts of Leuven far behind, I simply followed the old road and let her make the itinerary; a farmstead with a barking dog, soft meadows full of sweet-faced Charolais cattle, through dark stands of pine trees, where the wolf stood hiding behind a thick trunk, self-consciously picking his teeth with a dry splint of grass. A prickle of fear, then blessedly back to the sweet light-dappled hedgerows, and an entourage of pesky flies. To the left I saw a high conifer hedge, a neat gate and space for parking cars. Curious, I dismounted, pedalled the bicycle to the hedge and opened the gate.

It was a war cemetery. I was startled that I hadn't realised, but had been letting the meandering road take us where she wished. I resented being there initially, and wanted to take myself and my new life back to the light. The wolf had known in the pine forest; he was never to be trusted, as we are reminded once again.

Steeling myself, I placed my hand on my belly and began to walk down the first row of neat graves, then, compelled and taking onboard the vastness of the tragedy. The deeply carved inscriptions took my breath away with their collective grief:

Lieutenant Arthur Waverly	Born 1922.	Died 1942
Private Thomas Bridstow	Born 1919.	Died 1942
Private Ravi Patel	Born 1926.	Died 1942
Sergeant Scott Nolan	Born 1920.	Died 1942

They died near here, united in their sacrifice. Their homelands were Britain, India, the U.S.A., Australia, New Zealand and Canada. I walked on, they hovered all around me. Groaning, weeping and calling for their mothers, fathers, wives, brothers, sweethearts and unborn children. I patrolled the neat rows and became aware of my status as a pregnant woman carrying the next generation. I carried on like a visiting dignitary, with blessings and calm words to all the weeping young men. I felt their fear and their eternal homesickness, as they flickered in and out of the space in between. I brought them snapshots of their countries choked in motor cars and vibrant with democracy, of the outcome of WW2, of jumbo jets, men walking on the moon and rock and roll. I brought them shortbread biscuits and cups of strong tea, and told them how we appreciate all that they paid for with their short lives.

But I knew that the history books were tired of this war. And, as the last survivors staggered into the sunset, that these lost souls were very far from our collective hearts. New blood was being shed by a new generation of young men, egged on by cynical old men once more. I glanced at and acknowledged 10 by 65 rows of strong emotional disturbance. I was not afraid, more conscious of the role that I had to fulfill and to bear witness that they were still lost in action.

My unborn child and I passed by and addressed every grave, then returned to the gate, lifted the latch and walked back into the blossom filled world. The stricken young men rolled over on their sides and wept.

Recipe for Shortbread

A moment to pause and think, and the desire to never let war happen again. A handkerchief, a strong cup of tea and a shortbread biscuit are now called for. Take 130g of softened butter, 60g of sugar and cream together until fluffy. Add 130g flour, 60g of rice flour and (yes) a teaspoon of sea salt. Form the ingredients into a smooth dough. Preheat the oven to 170°C / 325°F / Gas 3. Using a 20cm loose bottomed cake tin, press the dough into the tin and smooth it down with the back of a spoon. Crimp the edges prettily using the tips of two fingers, then score the mixture into eight segments and prick each triangle three times with a fork. Bake for 30 minutes until it is pale golden, never dark. Remove from the oven and sprinkle with sugar.

13. Skillingsboller

September 1997

A fine cloud enveloped us as we stood at the front of the big iron ship, ploughing its way up the fjord to Bergen. We didn't care about the weather though, we were arriving in Norway with our precious cargo warm and nurtured under my unsuitable, and straining, Parisian jacket. Time enough for waterproofs in the next four years. But for now the thrill of being an anonymous pregnant woman, with a loving man by her side and a beautiful future ahead were the only shelter that I needed.

The physical shelter came along with minimum fuss and lots of luck in the form of a large, old wooden house perched high on the mountainside overlooking Bergen. Not so exclusive considering the city is surrounded by seven mountains to choose from, but definitely on the all-important sunny side of the city. The added attraction of this house was the roaring cascade that swept a carefully carved course through our rocky garden. After initial worries about the stream bursting its banks and sweeping us down the mountain, we relaxed and felt that it was safe enough. One other 'hidden' extra that did dampen our infatuation with the location was an eighty-six year old tyrant called *Lillemor* (Little Mother) who lived upstairs. Only my poor Danish man could understand her and bear the brunt of her petulant demands in upper class Norwegian, matched only by my own erratic and hormonal requests. Add a newly born baby girl two months later to these three stages of female life, and wait for the rains to fall and churn the stream into a torrent to muffle our demands.

The waterfall was no cruel howling water witch waiting for a sacrifice, though. Instead, a force of such power that the three wailing women had to be still. We all became quiet and listened to the strength and wisdom that the white water spoke of on dark winter nights. On the top floor of the creaking mansion, Lillemor tucked herself into her ancient marital bed and remembered her beloved husband. He, who had hewn the course of the stream from the hard black granite. He, who had built the beautiful Lillemor a warm and strong house to help cushion the memories of a Norway ravaged by the Nazis. And, indeed, her store cupboard in the basement remained still well stocked with long-past-their-sell-by-date tinned meats and biscuits, with faded lids of 1950s flowers, just in case the bad times came back again. There, in this solid and warm house, with the help of her straight-backed husband with his strong but gentle hands, she had seen her life being swept along with sweet sighs and laughter in her new wooden bed. The happy chatter of her fat children, easing her rationing fears and offering her a time of small joys. She rightly refused to leave her lofty house full of the ghosts of happiness, preferring instead her insomniac nights, pacing her memories in the long corridor of her life until the waterfall prepared to take her last breath away.

On those same winter nights that the old lady sorted through her dusty snapshots, I too would lie awake listening to the volume of the water rip through the rocky channel with the sound of a deafening jet engine. My baby girl invariably in my arms, I lay in the warmth and sweet fug of my little family's bodies. My mind would begin to process dark and unhappy images from my preceding years, but I never got very far. That swift and powerful force churning just a few metres away would sweep up my nagging fears and littered images, and whisk them away down the mountainside too. Some would return, streaked and nightmarishly distorted to haunt me in the quiet moments when baby slept and I gazed into the middle distance. But with a heavy week's worth of rain, the river goddess would overpower them and pull them deftly under the white foam.

Strip away the side of the wooden mansion and you would see us all as if in a toy house. On the first floor the little family of stiff-legged smiling and yawning new parents. Baby swaddled in muslin lying in her truckle bed made of a matchbox. The walls painted in a soft butter yellow, gleaming wooden floors and floaty curtains. Furniture made from lollipop sticks and cotton reels, all clean and covered in striped and chequered cloth. Mummy has made a chocolate cake and it sits on the cap of a cod liver oil bottle. The baby begins to crawl and mummy has much more padding up the front of her dress, and seems to be lying on the sofa a lot eating oranges.

The top two floors were occupied by Lillemor and we see her as a knitted doll with red lips and fine padded thighs. One day I'd been fumbling to find my keys at the front door and she had appeared dressed for a day out. I was staggered, the octogenarian was dressed in hot pants and a sparkling halter neck top, topped with a sun visor and huge cellulite riddled thighs. All I could summon up to say in my flaky Norwegian was,

Du er så vakker! (you are so beautiful). She accepted my compliment with a haughty nod and swept out of the house to get lost up the mountain for a day or two.

We spent two happy years in the warm wooden house. Our baby boy arrived and the long summer nights, as I pegged the elfin clothes out at midnight, were the essence of magic on our mountainside. I glanced up at our luminous house filled with all the things I loved the most, and knew that it was all much more than I could have ever anticipated. The palette of blues, greens, blacks and greys from the craggy peaks behind and around our home were our backdrop. We glowed with contentment.

Within a month of that dreamlike happiness we had to leave. Huge blowflies and the smell of decaying flesh became unbearable over a period of two weeks. I had visions of the old lady passing away, with her faded photo albums scattered around her pooled blood. Or else doing away with one of her infrequent home helps and Lillemor trying to hack her up and freeze her, just in case war broke out soon. Eventually we found out that the stench turned out to be from a freezer in the loft being left open and several packets beef burgers rotting. We were uneasy though, and the image of her fumbling with matches to light her stove began to flicker through my imagination late at night in the tinder dry wooden house, so we moved away down the mountain instead.

I always missed our little wooden home on the mountain though. In the winter of 2012 we took a visit down memory lane and visited the house. Incredibly the postbox for Lillemor still stood, and the same ragged 1950s curtains hung at the window. For all we know this feisty old lady is still ruling her kingdom and never did have that accident with matches.

Recipe for Skillingsboller

This recipe originally comes from Bergen, where my first two children were born. The name Skillingsboller means one shilling bread (sounds a bit pricey to me). The Norwegian way is to roll a huge oblong of the dough out and smear it generously with a paste of butter, sugar and heaps of ground cinnamon. This is then rolled up and cut into small rolls. The smell of the cinnamon always takes me back to our little wooden house on the side of a mountain, and our enchanted days in old Bergen.

Melt 150g butter in a very large lidded pan. Add 3 teaspoons of sea salt, 2dl sugar and 5 teaspoons of ground cardamom. Take off the heat and add 6dl milk, (the melted butter and warm saucepan will heat the milk to blood temperature), 75g of fresh crumbled yeast (or 2 teaspoons of dried yeast), and 2 eggs. Stir until the yeast is well blended. Add 900g of sifted strong flour and knead until it is all shiny. Put the lid on the pan and leave somewhere cosy and warm for 45 minutes, or until doubled in volume.

After it has risen to twice its size, knock back the dough and knead again until it is as smooth as a baby's bottom. Let it rest for 5 minutes and then roll out into a very large oblong.

Preheat the oven to 220°C / 425°C / Gas 7. Smear the 250g softened butter all over the dough, add 300g sugar and 2 tablespoons of ground cinnamon and squelch it into a rich paste on the dough with your hands. Roll it up into a huge Swiss roll. Cut in half, roll into a slimmer Swiss roll sausage shape, then cut into neat rounds and place on a baking tray lined with grease proof paper. Cook immediately for 20 minutes and transfer to a rack to cool. The second sausage may be rolled and cut as before, placed on a baking tray, covered in cling film and left to chill until you require it.

Another idea with the basic dough is to form small clementine sized balls of the dough after it has risen, and leave to prove in a warm place. Glaze with milk and bake at 220°C / 425°F / Gas 7 for 15 minutes. Divine served dusted with icing sugar and split with jam and whipped cream the English way, or the Danish way with jam and butter.

My latest invention is to put a couple of cubes of good quality dark chocolate into the small dough balls, seal them in and leave to rise. Cook for 15 minutes in an oven heated to 220°C / 425°C / Gas 7, dust lightly with sieved icing sugar and serve them while they are still hot…Yum!

14. Elderflower

June 1999

She spoke with an accent from another age. It was hard to get more isolated than living at the end of a fjord in northern Trøndelag, Norway in the early 1950s. And so, in the late 1990s when I caught-up with Rose in Bergen, her voice sounded more like it should be broadcasting on the BBC World Service, at a time when there still were pink patches of empire on the map. We became good friends, despite the 40 years between our ages. I became her special agent, adept at gleaning snippets of juicy information about new arrivals in our expat community. Rose wove the harvested snippets into a bright tapestry of our transient lives back at her home, which we called HQ.

Rose was a master of connecting and communicating with people. Always at ease with herself, she could work a room and get people feeling comfortable and accepted in record time. In turn, I became her student and she showed me how to open people up like flowers. After a while, together we could whistle our way through a crowded room and meetup a few days later to compare notes, then continue on our weaving and incorporation of all lose threads. Knots were tied off and new colours and designs always given consideration and thoughtful application.

In our long days of chat, strong tea and wise words she would occasionally cradle Kirsty, my first born daughter. After a short while, Rose would become nervous and eager to pass the baby back to me. Then one day, in the warmth of our industrious social activity at HQ, she began to talk about her life by the fjord and her dark days of homesickness for England and her parents.

She had been a young and privileged teenager during the war years in London. Her family had owned a large house in Hampstead, and they had watched bombs rain down over London during the blitz. At the end of the war, as Britain celebrated and the party ran on and on, she and her sister visited Norway where her older sister met and married a handsome young doctor. The following summer Rose fell for a blue-eyed widower during her vacation, despite her parents' anguish that both their golden girls would go north. She married her Norwegian and sailed her life towards the midnight sun. It was at this point that Rose stared into the middle distance and mentioned 'headstrong,' 'willful,' 'naïve' and 'you make your bed and you jolly well lie in it, by Jove!' Then she sighed and whispered wistfully,

'You see Alice, just after the war England was such fun.'

It was a couple of years later that we resumed the conversation. I returned to Bergen from visiting my parents, with two small babies in tow and an enormous suitcase filled with products from all the shopping in the UK. I'd sourced a bar of amber coloured *Pear's* soap as a gift for Rose, it smelled clean, pure and of another time. I confidently thought that she'd love it. Instead of smiling though, she looked away and sobbed quietly. Then she told me how she had continued stoically through her first long winters on her husband's farm, followed by no respite in the equally harsh summers, when millions of midges would descend in the three months of endless sun. She told how the local women had shunned her, for taking one of the few eligible men from their isolated community, how they had cursed her and uttered how she would never belong, and how she had well and truly sealed her fate by pegging her silk London underwear on the washing line. The dour church-going community gleefully passed sentence then; that she was an evil temptress come to wreak havoc on their mediaeval community, and that she would never ever belong.

Inside a small tin box on her dressing table she kept her precious bar of Pear's soap. When her homesickness would envelop her she would take the box and allow her mind the luxury to go home. The smell of the soap gave her glimpses of her family and the chatter of a London street on a summer's evening. The soap had been too precious to use to wash with; its aroma alone enough to bring calm and a small glimmer of sanctuary in her difficult life. Yet she underlined how she loved her husband very much, and her old eyes lit up when she cast her mind back to their early years. She giggled girlishly, and I had the feeling that the strong arms of her chosen mate were often enough to deflect the cold and dark that would have consumed many a weaker partnership. As time went by they became parents to a baby boy, her dismay at the coldness of the other women of the village began to fade as she created her own little universe. But with the premature arrival of her second baby, things turned dire. The primitive health care fell away in the middle of a very cold winter; all roads were impassable, and Rose and her sickly child had to make the dangerous journey to the nearest hospital over the mountains in a traction engine known as a *weasel.* Mother and child survived, but her obvious fear of holding my newborn baby was a result of the rising hysteria that marked her in those early days.

Rose was a thrifty and frugal cook, but she loved her food with abandon; her repertoire of 1950s and 60s recipes all carefully collated in a flip photo album. Inedible cakes made from crushed biscuits stirred into melted margarine, sugar and cocoa had me politely gagging. Her triumphant serving of instant soup made me smile, as it was such a joy for her not to have to make a soup from the beginning, meaning from planting the seeds. Rose had told me over the hot soup how, as a family, they had carefully stored all their potatoes, carrots and turnips in a root cellar below their farmhouse in the early autumn. But, by the spring thaw all the remaining vegetables had rotted into stinking slurry. In those intervening weeks, before the first shoots of radish began to show in the cold soil, Rose, her family and their neighbours would all show the tiredness, light headedness and bleeding gums distinctive of scurvy. The freezer, the microwave and most of all the convenience store all held such wonders for her.

Rose always inspires, nourishes and refreshes me with her insights and small glimpses of her remarkable past. Recently, she told me the tale of how she bought a spit-roasted chicken from her local supermarket, but had devoured it by the time she reached home ten minutes later. I see her staggering down a wet road with greasy lips, a chicken thigh in her hand and not an axe in sight.

Recipe for Elderflower Cordial

This recipe for elderflower cordial that I make every year. There is something frugal about it, which is also as precious and refreshing as Rose. I find it most successful to freeze the syrup; if you were to add chemical preservative to the mix it would be wrong. It's best made in the heady time of early summer, just as the elderflower comes into bloom and their perfume fills the air. As there is no cooking involved in this recipe, the delicacy of the flowers is retained, and even in the middle of a dark Scandinavian winter you receive the light kiss of a summer day.

Gently shake the perfect heads of 30 freshly gathered flowers to remove any insects. Place them in a large clean bucket with 3kg sugar, 6 sliced lemons, 40g of citric acid and 3.5 litres of cold water. Cover with a cloth and leave for 3 to 4 days. Stir and squeeze the ingredients at least 4 times a day with a clean arm. Strain the mixture through a fresh tea towel and pour into pretty bottles. This cordial should be kept in the fridge for no more than a couple of weeks, or frozen for a maximum of eight months.

This cordial is wonderful served with iced water, sparkling water, white wine, champagne or gin. The tiny flowers that escaped the straining process look beautiful floating in your glass.

15. Breakfast in America

June 2000

We had been living in Bergen for three years. A time of catching up with what people in their mid-thirties do. In between breaking world happiness records we'd also got married and I became Mrs. Alice Bonneville-Beck, we had two lovely babies and lived on the side of a mountain with an amazing view.

One rainy day my husband informed me how we could go on sabbatical to a university in southern California. Neither of us was too interested by the thought of uprooting again so soon, especially to the U.S.A. A diet of TV soap operas, bad movies, bullying foreign policies, guns and jealous rumours (from people who had never been there) had put the kybosh on the place for us. Coupled with that, I had begun to see the beauty in the boulders, pine and dripping moss of Norway. The soft watercolour nuances of grey, palest blue and white that covered the sky, and the soft rustle of raincoats in Europe's wettest city. I was content and safe on the nest in our rock garden. Our waterproof babies frolicked in forest glades, and I felt no inclination to look over the garden fence.

Luckily, the United States of America was great for my husband's work in code-breaking. He couldn't sniff at the opportunity to be there for his research. I reluctantly agreed, and dutifully packed our happy Norwegian life away and into storage. One wet July morning we fastened our seat belts, flicked through the in-flight magazines and just looked up in time to see the rocky outlines of Bergen's mountains disappear. Shrouded in veils of cloud, the brooding giants turned over on their hard beds. They tutted disappointedly, sighed and pulled the grey blanket higher.

Our flight passed through Chicago. Staggering through long tunnels to catch our connection to L.A. with wailing children, we sought strong coffee. The babies wailed louder and needed nappies changing and soothing creams applied to sore bottoms. Frazzled, I collected drinks and snacks from a self-service cafeteria and went to pay the young man at the checkout. Strangely, I'd suddenly become the leader and native English speaker. I liked it. I'd been silenced from speaking fluently for ten years in France, Belgium and Norway. This trip was looking up!

'Hi, how are you today?' he purred deeply, smiling widely with perfect meat-eating teeth. I was sure that I saw one of those glinting cartoon stars twinkle on.

All my preconceptions about American insincerity fell away in one huge rush of pleasure. He did it so well, totally confident and professional. All those doors that I'd had slammed in my face, all those hello's that were never answered, and all the nasty lack of manners that I'd forgiven the stiff Norwegians, the snobby Parisians and the elusive Flemish for, tucking them into a file named HURT. I beamed back at my new amour called America, and stealthily removed the ring from my sulky mountain home.

'I'm feeling great,' I replied earnestly.

'Welcome to the US of A, ma'am.'

I began to feel like a small stunted flower, uncurling in the sunshine of this young man's welcome. He pressed the iconic dollar notes, cents and dimes into my trembling hands. Then said,

'And have a nice day!'

With another glinting smile in place, he was attending to the next customer before I had the chance to tell him all about my plans for the rest of the day. But never mind, I was sated by his elegant welcome. The U.S.A. had bothered to put these manners in place, to seamlessly grease the wheels of a nation built from millions of people from all over the world. I was onboard and ready to mingle!

The next day we woke at some insane hour, staggered out of our air conditioned motel room to the heat of a San Diego morning and a local diner for my third taste of America. My well-travelled Dane immediately chose pancakes, maple syrup and bacon. I surveyed the menu for recognisable ingredients of my European upbringing, but drew a blank, and began to panic at the choice, quantity and weird combinations that the Americans gleefully ploughed their way though. A jaded waitress arrived and my husband ordered for himself and the chirping kids, then it was my turn and I ordered a boiled egg. As the words left my mouth I knew that I was an alien abroad. Some English twit that drinks cups of tea and says How do you do and Sorry and Oh bugger. The waitress simply couldn't understand me. I could have my egg over easy, easy over, snotty, grotty or squashed, but they darned well weren't going to do something as obscene as boiling it, then serving me with some toasted soldiers and a nice strong cup of tea. I realised that I was out of line and had it over easy with some watery coffee.

We had a fabulous time in the U.S.A. and my waistline and I grew to love the breakfasts. It really was just like looking over the garden fence and finding a place filled with humming birds, palm trees, swaying exotic flowers, charming inhabitants, loads of succulent food and a cloudless sky. Dour, but once-beloved Bergen was no match. We returned seven months later, in the insanely dark and cold month of January. I, the faithless wife, who had romped in bright sunshine with her hunky American, my brown legs parted as I kneeled in the golden sand laughing. I could no longer look in the eye all that I had once loved about the old place, it was obvious that I would have rushed back to the arms of America in an instant. It was time to move somewhere else. I began to re-pack my pink nylon negligee, ready for California, but Denmark beckoned with a professorship for my husband; I didn't understand how the world had become so suddenly small, and I'd lost my chance to chat once more.

Recipe for Breakfast in America

The memories of those perky and plump American pancakes keep coming back all these years later. My family starts squealing with delight when I suggest them as a breakfast item. The smell of them wafting up the stairs is sometimes the only way to get them out of bed on a dark Danish morning. I have tried American mixes from our local supermarket, pre-made versions and recipes off the internet, but all attempts failed and made my family suffer and the house stink. This recipe was given to me by my real American friend from Minnesota. Ironically, her ancestors were from the West coast of Norway.

Melt 2 tablespoons of butter in a frying pan. Meanwhile, sift 135g plain flour, 1 teaspoon of baking powder, 1 teaspoon of bicarbonate of soda, 1 teaspoon of sea salt and 2 table-spoons of sugar into a mixing bowl. Add 130ml milk, one egg and the melted butter and whisk lightly until blended, lumps are fine, as too much whisking does no good.

Wipe the frying pan with some kitchen roll to remove any excess butter and put it back on the highest heat. Once it is smoky hot, add a ladleful of the batter to the pan. Cook for a minute or so on each side, until bubbles appear. Keep the pancakes in a warm dish, away from thieving hands. Repeat until the mixture is used up and serve while still hot with maple syrup, butter and love. For once, all your family will be assembled and even teenagers will be sweetly appreciative of you and may even croak,

'Have a nice day!'

16. Flapjack

March 2004

The ground was sodden, the rich red earth littered with the stumps of bitten-down Brussels sprout plants. All was decay and sang a sad lament to the heavy grey sky. At the very top end of the wide field a girl with a blue hat climbs a gate, and takes in the harsh smell of rot and bleak scene. She gazes for a long time at the vast flock of crapping and chewing black faced sheep, until the sun gives up its miserable jaundiced light at four thirty. The girl walks slowly over to the sheep in the illuminated dusk, her boots slipping on the churned earth. The sheep cast wary glances, but stand their ground. She sings clearly,

'Do, re, me.'

The sheep stop chewing and gaze at her, an eight year old child with the voice of Julie Andrews. Three hundred ruminants are captivated. Never entertained before, they chew compulsively from side to side and piss a little. The made-up song of erratic falsetto notes pierces through the damp air. Then, abruptly the girl stops. She makes as if to run at the flock. They scatter to a distance of fifteen metres and wait nervously for the chorus. The chorus never comes. The child clambers back over the fence and slips from view. The sheep resume their dank grazing, as a curlew's cry cuts the desolation to the quick.

I changed the music and stared out of the window. Half a lifetime had gone by since I'd sung to sheep, but still the feeling of being a loner stalked my fears. Bach's cello took me away from the inadequate company of sheep to a Christmas spent alone in Paris a few years ago.

The self-contained child was coming unstuck. Outside the third floor window of number 16, Quai des Grands Augustins, the Seine rose to record levels. The child, now a thirty year old woman, gazed down to the seething brown water as it charged its way through the hardly defined arches of the Pont Saint-Michel. Even the old English tramp, who had been a permanent fixture in a disused doorway in a street nearby, had given up his normal habits for the company of comrades at the soup kitchen, or wherever the homeless at the turn of the 20th century went. She'd thought to offer him dinner and enter into the true spirit of Christmas, but her motives remained wrapped and the music of the cello squashed a little more air from her. The French friends that she'd cultivated were, as is the nature of big cities, from far flung provinces. Places that she would gladly have traded to get away from the cold stone heart of this brittle city. A walk, to walk away from this dark shadow that had followed her for so many years. Lipstick deftly applied, a haze of warm perfume and an emerald green cashmere cloak swirled on top. She quickly left the apartment in an attempt to evade the dark shadow. Clattering down the well-worn stairs, past the reeking *pissoir* of the *Bar du Vin* and out into the damp traffic-stained air. She was in awe of the city, the palette of grey winter light, the odours, the past casually walked upon and the superficial self-absorption of the present. The child with the blue hat had met her match. The shadow gave her a head start as she dashed across the busy road, trying to shake him off in the tourist crowds.

Ten years later. A baby cries from the adjoining room. Alice Bonneville-Beck, now around forty years old sits at the computer. She clicks on 'save', rises from the desk and walks briskly over to the crying infant,

'Is that my baby?' She murmurs to the kicking bassinet.

A small smiling face gazes up and any difficult memories evaporate. Milk begins to prickle in her breast and she lies alongside the rooting child, giving her sweet milk and soft words. Through the bedroom window the mother and child survey the misty February morning. The baby's satisfied cheek pressed to Alice's. She catches their reflection in the window and captures the moment forever. Mist sweeps across the garden in waves and last summer's foliage shakes in the light wind.

It never ceases to amaze me how good it felt to come home. To struggle through thirty years, that at times resembled a *Hieronymus Bosch* painting, with that dark shadow always adding the final ghastly flourish to every nightmare. To breathe steadily again and stare into the eyes of my three children and to know that those battles were over, and that there is an opposite of everything. I sit now in my high-ceilinged house; warm walls the colour of vanilla cake mixture, the smell of flapjacks baking in the oven for when my hungry children return. No time or space for the shadow, he can wait.

Recipe for Flapjacks

It feels a little mundane to offer you a flapjack to chew on, but these are so good and staggeringly simple to make. It's always worth remembering that the best ideas are the simplest ones: something that I never really grasped when I was younger.

Preheat the oven to 150°C / 300 °F / Gas 2. Line a square or oblong baking tin, approximately 30cm by 30cm, with baking paper. Melt 240g butter and 1tsp sea salt over a low heat. Add 240g brown sugar, 3 tablespoons of golden syrup and blend. Take the saucepan off the heat and add 360g of finely rolled oats and one egg. Mix thoroughly and the tip the mixture into the lined baking tin, level it lightly and cook for 40 minutes until just golden brown. The wonderful butterscotch aroma will waft around your home, making you appear to have been busy doting on your loved ones all day. Remove from the oven, cut into small squares immediately and leave the flapjack in the tin until it is cool.

17. Rice Pudding in a Duvet

November 2005

It's a popular myth that plenty of shagging goes on in Scandinavia. In the 1960s, British design guru *Terence Conran* capitalised on the concept that good-looking Scandinavians indulge in hot sex all year round. An advertising campaign featured a pouting blonde curled up, hot and naked in a downy double bedroll. Conran's feathered offerings flew off the shelves in record time from his swinging London store. Sex sells but, to be honest, the humble duvet is warm and cosy rather than hot. And in Denmark the best-selling size is single, like they have been for centuries.

Miserable weather, excellent insulation and icy stares are the real hallmarks of Denmark. The famously cold weather actually feels more like a grey horse-blanket, suspended over the sky for six months to steadily *drip-drip-drip.* The result is a dark, sun-starved and cold dampness that makes you want the country to close down and give up. But the cold stares from the populace, and their chronic lack of hospitable warmth is actually what makes living here such a chilling experience.

This is ungenerous of me, but also an observation gathered from painful experience. I didn't stand up for myself in the early days of living here. After being snubbed, treated roughly, and largely ignored as a foreigner, I chose to close down all integration initiatives for eleven years. I lashed myself to my children's international school like a lifeboat in a storm. I was, in turn, nourished by the wonderful cultural richness of the world in this environment, but actually living in a tiny compound outside the real village. It was a delightful place, where we all cared for and protected our happy children flourishing under a warm sun. We all found our homes again and against the backdrop of this halcyon existence rough Danish manners, or the lack of them, took a cultural-roasting in the flames of anger fanned by my unhappy expat friends.

With a population of 5.7 million scattered on the 406 islands between the North Sea and the Baltic, Denmark is a peaceful maritime and agricultural land. I should note that 24 million resident pigs are horribly treated by the smaller population of humans, a reminder that Danes are the descendants of vicious Vikings. People who have never lived here are quick to mention the Viking heritage, along with all that shagging, yet, it's worth remembering that many of the worst Vikings settled and spread their mean genes in the UK, Ireland, Northern France and Sicily. The clever agrarian, creative and mercantile members of the tribe remained here in Denmark. They whittled wood into signature designs, masterfully shipped trade goods around the world in their magnificent boats, and built great homes to keep out the crap weather.

Imagining modern citizens in Viking clothes fills my daily walks with piquancy and well-researched terror. The Danes are justifiably very proud, if a little in awe, of their scandalous ancestors, and have established well-planned and interactive Viking museums in the larger cities. A little while ago, soft autumn weather coaxed my kids and I back in time to Lejre Viking centre, just south of Roskilde. Like the open air *Frilands* museum near Copenhagen, it is a splendid hands on experience of historical and archaeological reconstruction.

We rolled up our sleeves for some half-timbered educational fun. Situated in a lush Danish landscape, its real hills thrilled us immensely in this monotonously flat land. We played roly-poly down them for half an hour. Dusting ourselves off, we were soon sitting in a Viking wattle-and-daub hut watching a broad-hipped wench forge a belt buckle over a charcoal fire. We moved on to a Stone Age village, where insolent, sooty, fur-clad children ignored us contemptuously. Next, we came to a hut of wolfhounds whose unstable-looking owners worryingly resembled their furry friends. We walked and walked and watched the autumn leaves zigzag down from the trees. But despite being happily married to a Dane, owning a house here and being mother to three half-Danish children, I didn't feel we were in the slightest bit wanted by the play-acting inhabitants. United by their shared heritage; their prickly hand-woven clothes, those blue-eyed stares, the Viking capes with exquisite bronze clasps and their finely sharpened daggers, they sent this message:

Watch and learn, but this is as close as you get. We are not interested in you or where you are from.

The dagger-like look was withdrawn and they sullenly continued to work. The cold reception that we received at every interactive homestead told me to beware and back off, and most of all to avoid any humorous spontaneity. I backed off and began retaliating in my mind's eye. I saw all our fellow visitors similarly attired in wolf skins and shapeless sacks, with sagging breasts and miserable once-handsome faces. Time stood still, and I was a captured Anglo Saxon thrall with my brood of blonde bastards; spat upon, buggered and bedraggled but never broken.

We didn't care that we weren't wanted though. We have lived here long enough to journey our berated way through thousands of years of flint, fire, feasting and *frikadeller.* A brief afternoon at this museum was a picnic by comparison. Or so I thought, until we turned due east and hiked past the sacrificial swamp towards some dugout canoes to reach an ancient beech tree. Suspended from its stoutest branches, a large dead stag twirled gently in the breeze. Its hind legs were tied with a noose and a fresh ruby-bright trickle of blood congealed on its nose. We walked past as stoically as the rest toward the demonstration of arts and crafts being held under that same tree. But I couldn't recover from the sight of the glossy mauve, green, and brown entrails deposited in a neat pile under the poor beast's gaping torso. My five-year-old stood for a good ten minutes gazing at the twirling stag. The huge antlers, gentle eyes and ruby-red droplet of life. The older kids moved squeamishly on to the pole-axed corpse of a goat; with its startled expression and flayed skin exhibited on an oak bench. A blonde *Valkyri* chewed on a roasted goat bone and spat at our weakness. I ushered the kids hastily on, just in time to see a nursery school teacher ask for a deer's skull for her class to carry home. The willing butcher began to saw happily through dry bone.

Now call me a sissy, but I come from the land of pre-packaging. Perhaps it is the result of the first industrial revolution happening in Britain, whereas Denmark had a more agrarian revolution. Though squeamish about butchery, I do salute the Danish cold-blooded approach. Many have hands-on experience raising livestock, and most cherish a tribal memory of killing them. In England, our agricultural past is more distant. We raise and devour an excess of flesh, but leave the slaughtering to others. I am respectful of the Danes for their bloodcurdling honesty about life, death, and dinner. But my son would not eat cocktail sausages with his fried eggs the next morning!

Exhausted, we made our weary way towards the timeless kinship of wood-smoke. The older kids wielded tomahawks with uncanny precision at pine logs. My yougest and I began grinding some wheat into flour with a stone and a quern. We achieved a handful of semi-decent wholemeal flour between us, mixed it with water, formed the dough into patties and slipped them onto an iron griddle. We were tired, so tired. But our four little cakes cooked to perfection. And just as easily as I had dismissed all Vikings, up stepped a gallant Danish dad. He shared his pot of honey, rendered our rough food edible and asked if we had enjoyed our day. We drizzled his caring words on our warm cookies and sighed with the contentment that comes from success in the fight for survival.

We returned home to my very own Viking husband, who had spent the Sunday alone and battling with the computer. He had been thoughtful enough to cook us his signature dish, Rice Pudding in a Duvet. A cunning, cosy, and very environmentally friendly homage to the land of great insulation, good husbands, short days, long nights and blunt manners.

Recipe for Rice Pudding in a Duvet

Place 2.5dl of water and 1 teaspoon of sea salt in a large thick bottomed saucepan and bring to the boil. Add 190g of pudding (broken) rice and cook for 2 minutes. Pour in 1 litre of full-fat milk and heat gently, stirring all the time. When it has reached boiling point, turn off the heat and place the lid on. The saucepan is then transferred to a quiet bedroom, placed on the bed and wrapped snugly in a feather duvet. Hopefully the kids, or you and your raunchy Scandinavian friend won't hop on the bed, at least for a minimum of four hours! During this time the rice pudding cooks gently, warms your duvet, and leaves you full of sweet anticipation. To serve sprinkle with ground cinnamon blended with sugar and a big blob of butter. Then forget your manners and gobble it as quickly as you can.

18. Nut Brittle

October 2007

The windswept island of Fanø, on the West coast of Denmark. A lazy Saturday afternoon in bright and icy winter sunlight. My Danish sisters-in-law and I stumble upon the high tide line, on the wide sandy beach near our rented accommodation. There were other people there, all ages and totally absorbed in gazing down at the sand. All were bent double and stirring the shadow of foam and dry debris from the sea with small sticks. I asked what they were doing, and a windswept lady opened her clenched hand to expose three small pieces of amber.

'Rav!' She exclaimed, with a crazed glint in her eyes. Then went back to her peculiar bottoms up posture and constant sand stirring.

To me, *Rav* conjured up another meaning. *Røv* (backside in Danish), but perhaps that is because I still laugh my head off at names like *Middlefart* (a town on the island if *Fyn*) or *fartmonster* (speedy car) or *fuld fart* (top speed) after all these years of living here.

We began with a bit of half-hearted stick twisting in the dried sea-weed, crab shells and broken fishing net. Within five minutes I had found a tiny grain of amber clinging gingerly to a clod of weed. I gasped and searched on. I've never been lucky with lotteries, tombolas, raffles or games of chance. I won't participate generally, as it is all too obvious that I have had to work hard for all the things that I treasure in my life. That weekend on Fanø turned the tables on me though, and five small nuggets later, I began to feel that I was patron to a charmed existence. Lady luck was in town, and for her I changed so much in the one frantic hour. I was ready to forsake my home and loving family, throw my keys, clothes, commitments and phone into the foaming ocean and try my feverish hand at fossicking for just one more stone. All this and attired in macramédd marram grass and living in a drift wood hut. The gulls cried, the sea roared and my old life faded into the greedy orange glow of the sun setting on the horizon.

Kun en mere (just one more) I pretended to joke to my amber-less sisters-in-law, as I drooled and imagined the fancy house I would build with round walls and an indoor swimming pool. I went back the next day, initially feeling more than a little ashamed at my faithlessness to nearest and dearest. Within a few minutes I'd gotten gold fever again, and was three darling nuggets up on the previous day's haul. I dragged myself away to the hungry, anxious faces of my children and we sped away across the vast beach in daddy's new (old) car. Well, we tried to, but we got stuck in the sand and had to be pushed out by seekers with tightly clenched amber-holding fists, and that soulless glint in their eyes. I bid farewell to gaudy lady luck, we caught the ferry from the island just in time and our youngest slept all the way home.

Recipe for Nut Brittle

I found similar sized pieces of amber to those I had found on the beach for sale in tourist shops, literally for peanuts. This recipe uses almonds, but makes a bounty of lovely am-ber-tinged treasure to share, without all the nasty side-effects.

Place 200g of whole unshelled almonds, 175g sugar, 1tsp of sea salt and 1dl water into a wok on a medium heat. As you heat the ingredients the sugar will become white, dry and crystalline. Turn the heat down low and keep turning the nuts with a wooden spatula, im-agining you are on a beach searching for riches. The crystallised sugar should melt and become a glossy brown. Turn the heat off, spread the almonds in a tray lined with baking paper. When cold, crack the nuts from each other and sigh contentedly that the recipe worked. I have personally ruined many kilos of lovely almonds in search of this perfect method, so please follow this hard-won recipe closely.

20. The Great Australian Bite

January 2010

A soft wind blew in from the Pacific. I stood away from my children, who ran giddily around the playground. The breeze kissed me, eased into my bloodstream and wrapped around my nerve endings. It smoothed its hot fingers softly over my hair and every once resistant part of me. I held my head up to accept the full embrace. I had never felt so well, so at one, and so at home. Sadly it was only for seven months, then back to dark Denmark.

Night comes swiftly in the southern hemisphere. Just before the final curtain falls, the soft flapping of huge fruit bats fills the air over our astonished heads. They make a nightly journey from the mangrove swamps to suburban Brisbane where they feast on fruit, flowers and insects. Once we hiked through scrub, eucalyptus forests and jungle and stumbled upon an overgrown cemetery, hacked out of the dense undergrowth. It frightened me with the intensity of its desolation, so lonesome and far away from the origins of those named on the slanting tombstones. Nature is felt strongly here. You feel her pulse. You touch her rich sienna soil, bleeding with minerals in the midday heat and are observed by a thousand unblinking eyes. You breathe the sickly smell of rotting eucalyptus leaves and the sweat pools on your panting lips, then walk on away from this place feeling disturbed, inconsequential and naive.

Australia now, is a strange mixture of the exotic, untamed, untapped, Oriental, European and the mundane. It could quite possibly not work, but it does magnificently with a style and confidence all of its own.

I'll start at the base of the continent, dry desert and scrub. Here lies the white hot heart of the land. An ancient impenetrable core where time is eternal and the old forces lie patiently waiting like a coiled snake. The white man seems happiest clinging gingerly to the rim, his feet in the sea and his houses placed in green grassed and orderly rows. The lawnmowers hum cheerily and children in school uniform skip up steps of modest homes in sunny streets. The metallic rasp of garden shears resounds. dad sings a jolly song and clips his ornamental bushes, while a funnel web spider weaves its wicked net in the undergrowth. The dark heart lurks in every garden, spinning silently and patiently. Australian dad copes well, lacing his leather boots to the knee and reminiscing about his fearless forefathers over a can of ice cold beer.

When we first arrived, streaked with tiredness, my husband and I walked out to the eerily buzzing darkness of the bush and were afraid for the first time. We'd heard too many scaremongering tales of toxic creatures great and small, all related by people who had never been to this continent. We covered each others every step and surveyed the environment like nervous New York cops. Within a few months we'd forgotten to be so frightened. Still, a strong respect for the other worldly nature tugged at my sleeve whenever something startling passed my way. New beasts were to be coped with. I'd read the local library dry on insect books and the history of the first white settlers. Surely the same nervous emotions were roused in the first white men reaching this land as in me? I bravely raised my vacuum cleaner nozzle over scurrying mouse sized cockroaches and closed my eyes. On all worrisome occasions, I brandished that same blessed suction at creeping and slithering creatures. One memorable night, I aimed it towards an evil beast hissing from our balcony. I cut the power when I realised the invader was just a fluffy possum mum and bug-eyed baby scrounging a snack. Their cries were alien, so foreign to our European ears. We were belittled, disarmed and overpowered by a fluffy marsupial.

I joined a writers' group in Brisbane. I'd meant to be so creative while my kids were in school. The opposite occurred, as I wrote only rich resounding letters home. I spent the rest of my time living my life with a vigour that had burst its banks with relief after my dour years in Scandinavia. The writers' group in Brisbane was peculiar, in that the eager grey-haired members were all writing historical novels. I was alone in describing the present. Australia seemed to be hurriedly writing its past, all effort devoted to establishing roots by academic means. I scribbled furtively in my A4 notebook, as my fellow writers eyed me suspiciously, rightly suspecting that vanity and continental luxury would lead me to write about myself, and them.

The bottom layer of Australia is the bedrock, the ancient bones on which the flesh of the place is borne. The middle layer is rich, loud and bursting with life and colour. No variations on shades of beige are found here. Picture then a massive cliff face made of sand and minerals blown to form a headland of unimaginable colours during the last ice age, the palette of inspired gods. Misty rain falls and a stream of the softest water bleeds from the base of cliffs that stretch for nine kilometres. The kaleidoscope escarpment towers overhead, coloured by fat and vivid layers of minerals. Costly shades of ochre, raw umber, burnt sienna, jasper, cadmium red and gold. A place of such energy, memory, beauty, and meaning: it was an epiphany for me. I felt myself falling through all past experience like a stone, and knew that I could now die an accomplished soul. I collected an ochre coloured piece of the soft rock from high up on the rainbow strata. When sacrificed to the eternal stream, the vivid colours infused the waters with heat and life. Other collected rocks of terracotta and deep red turned the spring water into a breathtaking miasma of colour from the dormant gods. The colours bled into the sea on the huge canvas of the beach. I bowed my head to the gods' power and knew in my soul that I could have stayed there forever, their worshipper, protector and artist.

Australia's top layer provides protein and the sustainable energy to ease the nation into the future with hope and optimism undiminished. I read long and hard of Australian history while I was there. I learned of the poor wretches on the First Fleet in 1788, the initial broken wave of 160,000 convicts transported to Australia, a jail with a wall 14,000 miles thick. I read of the genocide of the native Australians and the mistakes and mal practices of greedy and desperate men.

Yet, beyond the pages of pain and historical data, I found an adventure that left me breathless and staggered by the energy of the Australians. I remember hearing how the bodies of the first generation of prisoners were small and stunted from generations of poverty, abuse and bad diet. The first wave of bastard babies then grew into adults who were taller and better nourished, and thrived in the new settlement in Botany Bay. Vitamin D from sunshine gave them strong bones, and 'bush tucker' supplied fabulous nutrients. In English photos from the 1890s, the sitters look dead-eyed and already old; even the children are sad. When I peered at black and white photos of Australians from the same era, those pictured were smiling their heads off. They knew they were lucky people!

Recipe for The Great Australian Bite

I created this recipe in response to the variety, richness, health, and vitality of the place. There are three layers to the salad (I was only there for seven months) but you can add as many as you like.

Cook 5dl of basmati rice in 7.5dl of salted boiling water. Bring to the boil, cover and turn the heat down to the lowest setting for 12 minutes. Place the freshly cooked rice in a mound on a large, round dish. Place one roughly cubed aubergine, two red, two green and two yellow peppers sliced lengthways, one finely chopped red chilli, two large roughly chopped red onions and one roughly sliced courgette in a large baking tray, season with sea salt and black pepper and sprinkle nigella (black cumin) seeds over. Pour a good glug of olive oil over and coat all the vegetables by mixing with your hands. Cook in a very hot oven or grill until all the vegetables are roasted and sizzling. Turn the oven off and add the five chopped garlic cloves, mix around and place some baby cherry tomatoes still on the vine on top, place back in the oven for 5 minutes. Pile the vegetables and precious cooking juices on top of the mound of rice. Chop and crumble 250g creamy feta cheese and place on the salad, sprinkle fresh coriander over, squeeze one lemon over the salad and decorate with another sliced one. Finally, add a few healthy glugs of olive oil and freshly ground salt and pepper. Take the salad outside with some crusty bread, chilled Australian white wine and your best mates!

Take the salad outside with some crusty bread, chilled Australian white wine and your best mates!

20. Scrumpy

May 2012

American friends were set to descend upon my English hometown. I'd arrived with my children a few days earlier, and were happily installed with my parents in their little cottage. The church bells chimed eleven o'clock and I felt myself walk through the ghosts of many such mornings; lifting the latch of the garden gate and stepping into the gentle bustle of the old market town.

They were five in the American family, but I had the feeling that it wouldn't be a problem to find them some reasonable accommodation. But by one o'clock I'd knocked on the doors of every bed and breakfast establishment, only to be met by an apologetic,

'Sorry darling, we're full.' Followed by an optimistic 'Try the Ferry Inn!'

It was never a recommended destination, and as a teenager I'd avoided it like the plague. Often flooded in the wintertime, the Ferry remained a clammy lair for the local low-life all year round.

At the twelfth and final address I was once again turned away. But when mentioning the possibility of staying at the Ferry Inn, the landlady (a friend of my mother's) grimaced and replied in a broad

Herefordshire dialect,

'Oh, you don't want to be sending a dog there!'

'Still not good then?' I replied with a sigh.

'Yup, probably even worse than when you were a girl, more like bed and botulism' cackled the old lady.

Falling rapidly silent, we stood outside her spic and span guest house, folding arms defensively on heaving bosoms and looked ominously down the steep hill to the river.

'Hi, how are you?'

It was Bonnie, my American friend on the phone.

'Just to tell you that we've found somewhere to stay, somewhere called the Ferry Inn. It's reasonably priced and looks really quaint and olde worlde. AND there's room for us all with ensuite bathroom,' she chirped excitedly down the phone.

'Oh dear,' I replied sadly, picturing them with their perfect teeth and immaculate button-nosed children inspecting snail trails on the nylon carpet. There really wasn't much flexibility though, I'd tried my best, and the dank tavern doors grimly swung open to greet them.

Two days later Bonnie, her husband Bill and three spotless children arrived. It was a blue sky day, with high rolling clouds sailing over the green fields of Herefordshire from Wales. I walked with my rather crumpled children down to the river, then into the low-beamed tavern where we were met with a dark cloud of rising damp, spilt drinks and unwashed bodies.

In the gloom of the interior I spied a lone hunched form slowly drying a glass and painfully reaching to hang it up. He was illuminated by a sickly brown light; a silently flashing jukebox providing the only other focal point in the gloom. Drawing closer, my children hanging tightly onto me I called an over cheery,

'Hello, is this the right place for accommodation at the Ferry Inn?'

Feeling at once immensely protective of the kids and those well-raised friends from the United States I delved deeper into the nicotine stained darkness. A stifled squeal from my youngest as I engaged with yellowy eyes in a shaking and shrivelled nut of a face, it began to speak in a wheezy cough,

'Looking for the Yanks? Out the door and up the stairs at the back, room number 'free,' it gasped in a cockney accent with just enough air to get to the end of his sentence, and with a wheezing rattle flashed me a deathly smile. The mummified man stopped grinning in a flash, then replaced a smouldering cigarette on his crusted purple lower lip, and shuffled away through a greasy bead curtain.

It was only two nights, what could possibly go wrong in two nights?

With the children still hanging on tightly, we mounted a rather new staircase and knocked on the door of room number 3. It swung in and in the bright afternoon light we beheld the healthy and excited face of my beloved blonde friend, dressed fetchingly in jeans and white T-shirt. Framed behind her hovered the shiny offspring and kind-eyed husband, things were great, glorious in fact! The memories of the decayed man in the bar receded; the delight of the reunion, the order and newness of their room made everything good again. The children were overjoyed to see each other too, and were soon grabbing shoes and heading out to explore the riverbank.

'Say, shall we grab a beer?' suggested Bonnie in her soft Midwestern drawl.

'Say, sounds like a darned good idea' I replied, sounding more like John Wayne.

'Let's try the bar downstairs!' enthused Bonnie. 'I haven't been to an English pub before, it looks kinda creepy!' I bit my lip and hoped for the best, letting the children know where we were and heading into the darkness.

A woman now stood in the dingy light behind the bar, somewhat more in control than the shaking wretch who had given me directions earlier. She was tall, thin and dressed in an orange patterned dress from the 1970s. Aged about seventy years old, from under her tightly permed grey hair I saw sly eyes darting to and fro to assess the latest prey.

'What can I get you madames and mon sewer?' she crooned in a broad Croydon accent. Breaking into an insidious smile which exposed stained tombstone-like beige teeth; her eyes flickering with dancing greed and bony fingers drumming on the sticky pine bar.

'Hi, how ya' doing?' Bill enquired, the little quaver of uncertainty in his voice masked by that astounding confidence that Americans are taught in school. His sincere unlined face, casual shirt and newly washed jeans looked so out of place in this dive.

'I'm doing just fine young man,' she crisply retorted. 'Now what can I be getting you? We've got a fine range of beers, lagers and some very good local scrumpy.'

'Scrumpy? Apple cider? I like the sound of that,' enthused Bonnie.

'It's very strong, it's much more than just cider' I cautioned. 'It's a Herefordshire speciality, the real connoisseurs think it's best if you throw a squirrel in the brew for a more robust flavour.'

'Landlord! Three pints of your finest scrumpy, minus the squirrel' called Bill, sounding like Dick Van Dyke in his best Mary Poppins accent.

'Coming right up, and I'll join you if you don't mind,' added the old woman, as she coaxed the cloudy liquid from a large demijohn with a thick layer of shifting sediment in the bottom.

I felt a bit concerned, I'd grown-up with stories of old farmers going off on scrumpy binges in the woods. *It turns yer mind* was the general consensus of the village elders and only to be dealt out to the initiated.

We got stuck in, and despite it being at room temperature we were soon all happily slurping the appley beverage and munching on bags of chemical flavoured crisps instead of supper. The landlady rapidly threw her scrumpy down, wiped her mouth with the back of her hand, lit a cigarette, turning to the optics behind her and helped herself to a generous measure of Johnny Walker.

'I've 'ad an 'ell of a day' she confided. 'It's mi 'usband, he's as sick as a bleedin' parrot. More dead than alive he is.'

I had to agree, but really didn't warm to her, and looking into her eyes I saw tungsten steel pin pricks. My lovely Bonnie had the knack of being able to talk and facilitate most people, but I saw her blanch at times as the drunk and self-righteous old crone honed in on her, delighting in the subject of how useless and disgusting her old man was.

A young dark-haired woman entered through the beaded curtain. She cast an insolent glance at the guests around the bar, whispered in the old woman's ear and lifting a hinged hatch on the counter breezed through the room with disgust. I noticed that she met with four boys on revving mopeds outside.

'That girl is an absolute angel!' sighed the woman into the dregs of her evil brew. Tears misted her bloodshot eyes and she reached again for the flagon.

'Want another one?' she wailed.

'Sure, keep it coming!' cried an animated Bonnie. We were getting well-oiled and the swirling ferment wafted in and out of our now vacant minds. The children had returned to the inn, assessed correctly that the parents were jabbering idiots and had retired to the bedroom armed with ipads, flavoured crisps, chocolate, nuts and Coca Cola. All parenting had evaporating in the evil scum floating in the glasses of scrumpy.

The dark-haired girl returned and began a cursory wiping of tables and collection of our empty crisp packets. There were no other customers. She was about fifteen years old, wearing tight jeans, a skimpy top over swelling breasts and thickly coated makeup under her scraped back hair. She slipped under the bar and once again through the bead curtain, only to return and wordlessly take five bottles of strong pilsner from the fridge and outside to the moped boys.

The old woman lit a cigarette, turned to take another whisky and continued her rant from her stool behind the bar,

'I don't know what I'd do without Belinda. She's the light of my life that girl. Since mi 'usband took to the booze she's worked night and day to keep her old mum going! Selfless she is, just like me. What we've put up with from that old bastard's a diabolical liberty. Diabolical he is.'

I found *Jolene* by Dolly Parton on the jukebox and started singing loudly, Bill was dancing alone and Bonnie engaged in trying to solve the woman's copious problems and learning how to smoke. The scrumpy kept flowing and Belinda emerged once more through the greasy bead curtain wearing a large python around her neck.

'Would you look at her, she's like Salome tempting John the Baptist!' cried the crone appreciatively as her daughter began languorously draping the drowsy snake on poor Bill's shoulders. Fortunately, just at that moment a white BMW with dark windows pulled up outside the open pub door. Techno music throbbed loudly, and the moped boys started milling around like excited puppies. White-faced Bill was relieved as Belinda abruptly lifted the 10kg python off him and averted it from continuing to flex its coils around his alarmed body. Snake and girl ducked under the bar and through the mysterious curtain, while Bill muttered something about changing his underwear and Bonnie and I asked for a cigarette.

In hindsight we should have got out of there at precisely this point, but were drunk on scrumpy and the unfolding theatre. Bill returned wearing new trousers and went to put *El Paso* by Marty Robbins on the jukebox. The mummified man reappeared and painfully fought off the bead curtain, four fat blowflies accompanied him into the bar area. The landlady swivelled round on her stool, and with cigarette held high shrieked,

'Get outta 'ere! You'll frighten the guests and you're making the breakfast early, s'my night tonight!'

The wretch seized his chance, grabbed a glass with great agility; pressing it under the forgiving ministrations of the Johnny Walker optic several times before scuttling painfully away.

'Scrumpy pleashe,' I drawled to Belinda, who had tactfully replaced her cursing mother behind the bar, and who now sat with us, I handed her a crisp £20 note. Three more pints, a bag of nuts and a fistful of change later the till rang shut. Then, squarely blocking her mother's view from her barstool Belinda lightly pressed the drawer again, slid her right hand into the cash tray and extracted the uppermost notes. Without glancing at us she slipped the money into her inside sleeve, picked up a tray, ducked under the bar and out through the inn door.

'An angel, a beautiful loving angel she is,' dribbled the old woman into her whisky as Belinda opened the door of the white BMW and it drove away.

The next morning a ruffled Bonnie lifted the latch of my parents garden gate and informed me that they'd checked out and were leaving immediately. I grabbed my shoes and she explained as we walked back to the inn that the shrivelled man had indeed served breakfast for them. She'd been unable to eat it as dandruff rained down on her fried egg and bacon, his delirium tremens was so bad that he spilled most things anyway. Somehow their sense of propriety and manners had still held them back from complaining. Their frayed patience finally snapping when the shrivelled man had shakily served Bill with a cup of black coffee, a blowfly silently swimming in the bitter brew.

Recipe For Scrumpy

Scrump about 10kg of a variety of apples from the gardens of friends and neighbours who don't know what to do with them, the hedgerow (not tiny crab apples) and, if all else fails the supermarket. Wipe them lightly if needed, remove any rotten bits, leaves and slugs. You do not need to core them, but they should be roughly quartered and crushed into a coarse pulp first - I find that a normal kitchen Magimix works well for this.

Find somewhere outside to work, pressing is a really messy business, then get yourself two square boards. Line these with clean tea towels and place the pulp on one of the boards and make a wooden sandwich by putting the other board on top . Using G-clamps – or even a bench vise – squeeze till the juice runs out. Collect the juice – a lipped tray is useful for this. It's best not to rush the process as the juice, after the first lovely rush, will be released slowly requiring a turn of the screw every five minutes or so. I manage to get about 5 litres of juice from 10 kilos of apples. Collect the juice into a clean bucket, then pour it through a funnel into the demijohn and right up to the top. Do not add sugar or anything else. Place in a cool undisturbed place and leave the bung off - traditional cider making relies on wild yeasts and the air through the top will allow them in. The cider should start to foam in a couple of days. Wait for several weeks until fermentation stops and then replace the bung. If the fermentation doesn't occur don't give in to the urge to add a squirrel!

Leave your scrumpy cider to mature for at least six months – if it has gone wrong it will have turned into cider vinegar, If it has worked, you get strong, still and slightly cloudy cider. Before consuming a lot of it hand over your car keys to someone you trust, lock the doors and send the kids on a play date.

:nmark, junior realised that it was indeed her moment to inter-ne. At heart she couldn't really believe that she could stumble from r warm bed and be given Alice senior's full attention. But after six onths of her weeping, followed by the past few weeks of continual ıdy and calm, things were looking promising.

.ke all things in my life, every time Alice was thrown in at the deep ıd of the swimming pool. The shock of the cold is the worst part, ıt I often wonder in retrospect why I don't try wading through the ıallows first? As usual there was no time to think, only to surface, read water and adopt a doggy-paddle to reach the side of the pool. quick towel dry, and then time to greet the first batch of tourists.

hovered nervously behind a potted palm in the reception of a modest ıotel. My sixteen travellers filtered in, and I observed them chatting weetly amongst themselves. They were a mixed bag of middle-aged rish couples on a whistle-stop tour of Scandinavia. I suppressed my nowledge of all the horrible deeds the English had inflicted upon heir nation in the past, and waded in with an outstretched hand and an open smile.

I really needn't have worried; they were wonderfully kind and generous people and we parted, and hugged like old friends at the end of the three hour trip. AND we were in my favourite Danish town of Helsingør, or Elsinore as Shakespeare renamed it. The massive fortress of Kronborg standing guard of the sound between Denmark and Sweden, and the huge car ferries surreally looming over us. The frenetic view worked its special magic on my windblown Irish group, and my storytelling began.

This crossing has always been busy. If you drag your hands through the shiny pebbles on the beach you will uncover a fistful of sea-worn treasure. From softly sandblasted glass fragments of dark green, royal blue, turquoise and brown, to terracotta jug handles, tiles, red bricks, patterned plate fragments and chipped memories of rustic mediaeval faience-wear. Last summer I was lying on the beach making pictures of

21. The Archaeology of Ap

February 2013

It took three weeks to devour all the Danish history
in English. One week later I'd done a machete job
the Danish books in my local library. A friend with a
had recognised me as a budding tour guide, and ou
had offered me a job. It felt like a glorious coming to
things 'Alice', the essence of a much younger me. Ther
twelve, armed with a torch, a teddy, and the whole nigh
eclectic cocktail of information; diatribes on the social c
Victorian servant girls, of Roman soldiers relish of rotte
and of Mesolithic hunters' painting on cave walls.

This Alice had been put aside for many years. She'd be
through art school, dressed-up like a clown, she'd had
auburn hair shaved off, she'd put up with a huge cast
boyfriends, and she'd had to talk in front of thousands a
scarves on handbags in Paris. Alice junior had never been
about any of this, and was scornful of the erratic beha
she did see merit in experience. With Alice senior stric
the rollercoaster ride plummeted into an unfriendly smal

Denmark, junior realised that it was indeed her moment to intervene. At heart she couldn't really believe that she could stumble from her warm bed and be given Alice senior's full attention. But after six months of her weeping, followed by the past few weeks of continual study and calm, things were looking promising.

Like all things in my life, every time Alice was thrown in at the deep end of the swimming pool. The shock of the cold is the worst part, but I often wonder in retrospect why I don't try wading through the shallows first? As usual there was no time to think, only to surface, tread water and adopt a doggy-paddle to reach the side of the pool. A quick towel dry, and then time to greet the first batch of tourists.

I hovered nervously behind a potted palm in the reception of a modest hotel. My sixteen travellers filtered in, and I observed them chatting sweetly amongst themselves. They were a mixed bag of middle-aged Irish couples on a whistle-stop tour of Scandinavia. I suppressed my knowledge of all the horrible deeds the English had inflicted upon their nation in the past, and waded in with an outstretched hand and an open smile.

I really needn't have worried; they were wonderfully kind and generous people and we parted, and hugged like old friends at the end of the three hour trip. AND we were in my favourite Danish town of Helsingør, or Elsinore as Shakespeare renamed it. The massive fortress of Kronborg standing guard of the sound between Denmark and Sweden, and the huge car ferries surreally looming over us. The frenetic view worked its special magic on my windblown Irish group, and my storytelling began.

This crossing has always been busy. If you drag your hands through the shiny pebbles on the beach you will uncover a fistful of sea-worn treasure. From softly sandblasted glass fragments of dark green, royal blue, turquoise and brown, to terracotta jug handles, tiles, red bricks, patterned plate fragments and chipped memories of rustic mediaeval faience-wear. Last summer I was lying on the beach making pictures of

21. The Archaeology of Apple Pie

February 2013

It took three weeks to devour all the Danish history books written in English. One week later I'd done a machete job on many of the Danish books in my local library. A friend with a travel agency had recognised me as a budding tour guide, and out-of-the-blue had offered me a job. It felt like a glorious coming together of all things 'Alice', the essence of a much younger me. There I was aged twelve, armed with a torch, a teddy, and the whole night to read an eclectic cocktail of information; diatribes on the social conditions of Victorian servant girls, of Roman soldiers relish of rotten fish sauce and of Mesolithic hunters' painting on cave walls.

This Alice had been put aside for many years. She'd been dragged through art school, dressed-up like a clown, she'd had her lovely auburn hair shaved off, she'd put up with a huge cast of unlikely boyfriends, and she'd had to talk in front of thousands about tying scarves on handbags in Paris. Alice junior had never been consulted about any of this, and was scornful of the erratic behaviour. But she did see merit in experience. With Alice senior stricken, after the rollercoaster ride plummeted into an unfriendly small town in *cloud galleons with my youngest daughter, then casually remarked that I knew that I would find some treasure. Minutes later, as I drowsily dredged the stones behind my head, I came upon a twisted pewter spoon. The story lies so close by on this energy-charged shore. This place where we sweetly lay was composed of moments of time. With every turn past the red brick battlements or whitewashed interior dungeons, you feel you would have glimpsed someone a second earlier. Layer upon layer of lives, all churned by the constant tide and scattered across the beach. You just need to know how to look.*

Good! I noted with relief that the group weren't at all fazed by my flowery descriptions. We turned our backs to the bitter wind and headed away from the fortress.

The town of Helsingør is bursting with stories untold. Modern day tales begin immediately as you close your eyes and hear the jolly rattle, jingle and thump of beer crates being pulled on trolleys across the old cobbles, as day tripping Swedes hastily purchase cheap Danish booze to take home to their prohibition-ridden land. Summer café terraces are filled with their drunken countrymen, as they dribble into their beer and marvel at the salacious nature of cousin Denmark.

My tourists really were enjoying my storytelling, but they began to look longingly at the cosy bars. A quick glance at the outrageous prices had them taken aback and basking in indignation. But I understood their desire to find a cosy place to defrost, it was terribly cold, with a wind chill taking the temperature down to minus 18°C.

Helsingør is situated on a very cold and draughty corner, between the Kattegat and the Baltic. Even in Shakespeare's Hamlet the extraordinary cold is referred to twice.

I knew why he emphasised it. Snow flurried around us as I battled to get the words out, and I realised that it was vital that I should abandon the sightseeing and keep my sweet Irish group alive and happy. We scurried up one of the straight mediaeval streets, as I was thinking of my favourite café; the strong hot coffee, delicious cakes and my table in the corner. On either side of us stood stately brick merchant houses, with glimpses of warm interiors and a flickering candle. Grandly wrought facades of embassies from the 17th century nestled inbetween more modest half-timbered taverns and chandlers. Underneath the grand old bones of these once noble buildings were garish liquor shops and discount stores. Helsingør has declined since its heady days as the Dubai of the renaissance times. She was, after all, the spoilt mistress of a very lucrative idea indeed, which spanned 400 years. In a sheltered courtyard I gauged the spirits of my group and began to tell them the origins of this faded splendour.

During the last quarter of the sixteenth century, Denmark was the most powerful continental kingdom in Northern Europe. The reasons for this rise to wealth, riches and fame were conceived one hundred and fifty years earlier by a young king, named Erik of Pomerania. Fifteen year old Erik had the dizzy challenge of finding himself as the sole ruler of the United Kingdom of Scandinavia; Denmark, Norway, Sweden, Finland, the Orkney Islands, the Shetland Islands and Schleswig Holstein in Northern Germany. A huge swathe of far flung lands, that became immensely costly with the expenses that were incurred to rule them. Previously, huge shoals of herring had more than adequately filled the royal coffers, but these oily fish had mysteriously slipped out of the hands of the Danes to move elsewhere.

I was losing my audience. Some of the more elderly people began to crumple and glaze-over. I made one last attempt to serve them the frozen mists of time.

Young Erik tackled his changing fortune with genius. In 1423 he summoned a group of merchants from the powerful Hanseatic League, and informed them of his cunning plan. An idea so brilliant that it has been described as 400 years of legal piracy. Erik informed them that henceforth he intended to levy a new toll; every ship wishing to sail past Helsingør would have to dip its flag, strike its topsails and cast anchor so that the captain might go ashore and pay the customs officers in the town. Naturally, the horny crew would disembark and spend their time and money in whorehouses and taverns. Supplies would be replenished, ropes and sails mended, the butcher, the baker, the candlestick maker all visited. Often the paper work would take weeks! The final flourish of this scam was that the ship captains would then have to wait patiently for the right wind to fill their sails. It seemed like Erik had it all thought out.

That was enough of that for the reluctant historians. We staggered on through the blizzard in search of shelter and my beloved bakery. We arrived to find the pretty old-fashioned frontage smashed and in the process of being gutted. After 155 years the business had been sold to a steakhouse chain. I'd felt that a visit here would be a fitting and off-beat end to my first frozen tour. In the old days, as they'd now suddenly become, the baker himself would mingle amongst the clientele of day trippers and frail old ladies, just as his great great grandfather had before. Sometimes he would offer us a stale meringue called a *Kys*. He would blush when I laughed about him offering me a kiss, and didn't know that he had been funny. One day he wandered amongst us enjoying the polite laughter and smiles of his guests, not finding out until later that he had a small lump of dough with a raisin on his long nose. To me the passing of this small slice of history is a tragedy. Another bright ribbon is snatched from the hair of the once beautiful mistress of Kronborg. I grieve that I never photographed or sketched the coffee cups rattling, the arthritic old ladies with splendid hats, the 1950s décor and my pink-cheeked tourists, defrosting over hot coffee and cream cakes. We found a nice warm bar instead.

Recipe for Danish Apple Pie

I can offer you an edible memory; a slice of cake that is devastatingly simple to make, charming and delicious to savour. Perhaps inspired by generations of frozen visitors and inhabitants seeking solace, warmth and some famous Danish *hygge* (cosiness) in this icy northern land. Serve the warm cake in flickering candlelight with a large dollop of crème fraiche.

Heat the oven to 160°C / 325°F / Gas 3. Take 100g butter and melt it gently in a medium-sized pan. Add 175g sugar, 100g plain flour, 1tsp baking powder, 1tsp sea salt, 40g desiccated coconut and 1 egg. Beat with a wooden spoon for about a minute, until blended. Line a small cake or flan tin with baking paper and dollop the cake mixture in. Peel, core and cut two apples into thin segments. Lay in a spiral pattern over the flattened cake mixture. Sprinkle with two dessertspoons of sugar and ground cinnamon, and sigh at the speed and simplicity of the recipe. Bake the cake for about 40 minutes, or until an inserted knife comes out cleanly and your house is haunted with the wonderful smell of apples, cinnamon, history and love.

22. Hot Dates

October 2013

Deeply sweating tarmac, that greets you with a belch from the oh so civilised airport terminal. The bright rear lights of luxury cars glow fat and seductive under the velvety blue sky. Our charming driver appeared clad in a long white *kandura* and perfectly ironed head scarf, his immense belly propelling us proudly towards the waiting limousine.

So began a time of change and bitter-sweet culture shock, as the Emirati people of Abu Dhabi proudly showed us their land, and extended their welcome beyond anything we had ever experienced before. I would say that it was humbling to watch and learn the grace in which this nation treats its guests.

It was startling to open the thick hotel curtains the next morning. Outside lay a totally man-made view; high ultra modern buildings piercing the heat haze with a show of courage, sometimes stupidity, and wealth that no celebrity architect could resist. That night I dined on a trio of tiny scoops of sorbet with a pretentious decoration of shaved, cracked and drizzled chocolate. It looked similar to the architect's garnish of cultural mayhem that money can sometimes provoke in normally self-respecting people. But it was an outrageous, bold and loaded sight. It needed study, as people seemed solely hell-bent on raking in the money. Unselfconsciously exhibiting little regard for the past, the future, taste or conscience.

We drove in a taxi past the huge Grand Prix racing circuit on Yas Island. Its massive roof blinds, to shield the relentless sun, made me think of the same design in ancient Roman amphitheatres. The difference in function between the racing track and the gruesome gladiatorial games being very close; to entertain a wealthy and bored population with blood, gore, glamour and adrenalin rushes. Perhaps this land is similar to ancient Rome? Maybe one day goats will roam around the scattered girders and detritus of these iconic buildings, and the desert will once again rule and wipe away this moment in time. I could feel the recent impoverished past of this emirate rubbing shoulders with this age of Midas; laughing and grinning like a child at the sheer folly and exuberance that money has bestowed. What a treat for an arid place to rise up beyond the wildest dreams of its grandfathers and become the single richest city on earth!

But who built it?

The answer is startling. Abu Dhabi's 420,000 citizens, who sit on one tenth of the planet's oil and have almost $1 trillion invested abroad, are worth about $17 million apiece. The rest of the population is made up of both a million western employees of the petrochemical business and associated trades, but also a staggering amount of poor migrant workers from places such as Bangladesh, Pakistan, Nepal, the Philippines, Thailand and India. You could see the small white buses filled with these workers, who physically built this metropolis, as they cross the sleek black highways on Saadiyat Island to their dismal shanty towns beyond the city limits. Their fatigued gazes begged for love, home and family. But enduring a two year work stint, with often their passports confiscated, perhaps their survival was the only wealth that they could hope to take home.

It was the balance of genuine goodness and terrible money-driven evil that created such a dilemma with this city for me. The cruelty of human nature, which you could hope was left in the far distant past, was thriving under a hot sun as we frolicked in the pool. I'm ashamed to say that I began to look the other way. I glanced at the headlines in the local expatriate newspaper in-between rubbing sun cream into my lucky children's white skin.

Abu Dhabi. A woman jailed for 13 years for sexually assaulting and beating her maid to death, claimed she died by accident, reported the daily expatriate newspaper.

Two Asian window cleaners died yesterday after their platform fell from the 15th floor of a building on Khalifa Street in Abu Dhabi.' The newspaper added that '*..the platform had hung by one cable for three hours, before plunging the un-named men to their (uninsured) deaths.*

My head was very turned, and then my heart followed. My conscience berated me, but she would have to wait her turn. I hungrily tuned in with the timeless mystery, sensuality and exoticism of Arabia. Heady delights for all the senses, the sound of the imam calling the faithful to prayer in the pink dawn of the day. The pungent perfume of oud wood burning in tiny golden braziers, filling the air with a thousand sighs and secret glances. Teenage girls at the shopping mall wearing the traditional black costume, then sitting on a bench nursing their sore feet, after an afternoon spent pacing the malls on seven inch Union Jack stilettos.

We were showered with gifts and warm hospitality. We struggled with trying to find the right clothes to respect their modest dress codes. One night in particular stands out, when my children and I descended to the marble foyer of the hotel to meet an Emirati friend of a friend. She arrived in her black *abaya*, swathed in perfume and exquisite make up. My 9 year old daughter was dressed in a long Singapore airlines costume. My 14 year old daughter in a traditional green Emirati kaftan and golden headpiece. My 13 year old son in long shorts, tea shirt and baseball cap, and myself in an Indian long sleeved blouse and baggy pants. As we entered a mirrored elevator with our Emirati friend in black, I laughed at our reflection and remarked on how we looked like a delegation from the United Nations, we looked fabulous!

Recipe for Chocolate Covered Dates

Sad to say that our taste buds were not as overwhelmed as our other senses during our stay. The majority of food on offer was Indian, Thai, American or Italian. There was barely a whiff of the traditional Arabic cuisine; its deep roots in the plentiful use of spices, fish and a heavy reliance on the wonderful local dates. This recipe is my interpretation of a beautiful combination of date, nut and chocolate. True, we first tasted them from the duty free shop on our way home.

Take a small saucepan and half fill with boiling water, turn the heat on to keep the water simmering. Place a glass or metal bowl on top of the water, break 200g of best quality dark chocolate into small pieces, tip into the bowl and melt slowly. Toast 150g of whole almonds under a hot grill. Take the stones from 400g of fresh dates by slitting them with a sharp knife, and then stuff each date with a whole toasted almond. Re-shape the date, stick a skewer into it and coat in the chocolate by twirling it around in the melted mixture. Place each dipped date on the baking tray, take the cocktail stick out and leave in a cool place to set.

These are absolutely divine. Rich, satisfying, exotic, sensual and almost healthy!

23. A Piece of Cake

January 2014

Treading quietly through the empty house. It smells of warm wax, and the first tender fragrances of the buttery cake baking on the oven. A ticking clock chimes, and I await my children's return home from school. I fill the kettle and always give a thought to England at teatime.

I fly across the brown winter fields of Denmark, to the patchwork of my homeland. Lovingly tracing the outline of the A40, my ghost road. It twists its geriatric way through Herefordshire, en route for Pembrokeshire and the grey Irish Sea. It starts, or ends, in London, where it roars and stinks, and is the alter ego of the kindly winding road that deposits me at my parents' door in Hereforshire.

My ghosts lie in wispy layers. Quick sketches of moments, they disperse with the passing of time and the heavy traffic of my mind. Some fluttering with plastic rags on skeletal trees. Others dance skittishly with a chorus of trash and leaves, as the draught of a car passes and rouses them to a frenzy.

Moments on the journey home flash and blaze, as I gently place four china teacups on a tray. The good schoolgirl, with purchases from her piggy bank of sparkling plastic and nylon fur; all the things to snip, model and glue on a rainy Saturday afternoon.

The student, hair curled and too much makeup on, sits on the top deck of a lurching bus, wondering sulkily why the young can't have lots of money to spend.

The crying twenty-year-old, bitten-down nails grip the steering wheel. So sad-eyed, so bleached blonde and hurting badly. Lost, but going home on automatic pilot.

The artist's muse, a beat-out car and a black eye subtly disguised with a smudge of dark brown powder. Why did nobody ever see the fear beneath the pretty bones, and why did love have to hurt this much?

The glamorous thirty year old, brightly wrapped gifts stuffed into expensive bags. A veil of perfume, crimson lips, a shadow of sadness concealed and a hint of wine stain on the teeth. Unbeknown, the biological clock is primed.

Recently, the mother with her jet-lagged babes. The road leaves the Severn valley and begins to climb in hairpin bends, to the softly rounded limestone outer reaches of the Forest of Dean. At this point I gently wake the children to show them my secret kingdom. Their airport eyes adjust to the lushness of the trees and the tremble of fairy wings. Four thirty on an early summer morning. No other cars, but wild animals brazen in their early world. Fox tail flicking into the bracken, dopey rabbits warming on the tarmac, raven ripping last night's road kill from the cat's eyes. We intrude like sleepwalkers into a pristine world.

I pour boiled water into the teapot. My eldest daughter is the good schoolgirl now. I'll watch her well, but let her go and find her own way home. I'll be there waiting for her to climb down from the bus. I'll not hug her in front of her teenage friends and I'll continue to struggle with letting her go.

Today I will give all the children a slice of their loving heritage. A cake with a taste so very British it should receive a knighthood. I will make it carefully today, as when I am not serene (which I'm not today) then it shows in my cakes; with burnt crusts, a sagging middle, dried-out texture, or too much baking powder and an inflated exterior. I hope that at least tastes good and lets them know, just a little, how much I miss them.

Recipe for Victoria Sponge Cake

Turn the oven to 180°C / 350°F / Gas 4. Line a 20cm round cake tin with baking paper. Take 250g of softened butter, the same of sugar and the same of eggs (about 4) and place it all in a large mixing bowl. Sift in 250g soft cake flour, 2 teaspoonfuls each of baking powder and vanilla sugar and beat until light, fluffy and creamy. Transfer into the lined cake tin and bake for about 40 minutes. Check the cake by inserting a sharp knife, if it comes away cleanly then it is done. Once slightly cooled, take out of its tin and transfer to a wire rack to let it let off steam.

When it is cool, cut the cake horizontally through the middle with a bread knife and sandwich together with loads of raspberry or strawberry jam. Dust with icing sugar and place it on a pretty plate. We love it with hot custard sauce and a pot of tea at 16:00, the same time that Queen Victoria used to take her afternoon cuppa' and a piece of this cake.

24. Müesli

April 2017

Hiking steeply uphill, every part of my body working, like a fine-tuned machine. The air at 2000 metres was thinner, causing me to stop frequently. While catching my breath, I listened to the delicate spring overture that was developing all around; the excited chatter of streams filled with meltwater from snow fields higher up, the invisible birds that sang their distinct spring melodies of love, and the sweet wind gently tousling my hair, rattling the dry grasses and high pine boughs all around. It felt pristine and that I was the first woman in the world.

The snow had all but disappeared on the forest floor, and with every resounding footfall on the rough track, I became aware of my senses alive to the steady pulse of Mother Earth. Heart beating bass, with noisy thoughts and fears softly bathed and left swaddled and still. No other human sounds; no roar of cars in the bottom of the valley, no vapour trails and distant rush of a jet engine in the sky. The friends that I'd travelled with were out skiing with other tourists on the distant pistes, the Swiss people of the town tended to the visitors and their children were all in school. I was the sole human on this mountain, and fell into the soft caress of the awakening land.

I wore yoga clothes, my daughter's rucksack and some cracked winter boots. The only sane piece of equipment that I had was a free map that I'd picked up at the tourist office. It had led me to a signposted track which gave a blessed normality to my wandering the Alps without anyone knowing where I was. Higher up, I stumbled upon a sunlit glade. It was around midday and I felt ravenously hungry. Several hours had passed since I'd eaten a big bowl of müesli at breakfast, and had woefully underestimated the energy that you burn at high altitudes. Positioning myself in the dappled sunlight, I unpacked a lunch of a banana and an apple stolen from the hotel buffet, plus a packet of nuts and a litre of creamy milk from an over-priced Swiss supermarket.

Those were the first precious sunbeams of the year, after six months in the desperate gloom of a Scandinavian winter. I rolled the legs of my yoga pants higher, but pulling my jumper off felt like it just wasn't enough. The songbirds called to their mates, golden eagles wheeled on the thermals over the Eiger in a cobalt blue sky, and flies clumsily took their first flights. All alone but so connected to the steady breath of nature, I took off all my clothes, submitted to the sun and lay down on some dry moss.

Meditating, aware of all the delicate sounds around me. Fragments of bliss seeping through my bloodstream and running strong fingers over my body; my mind still and body anchored in the earth. The sun began to tilt to the right, and stretching luxuriously on the fragrant bed I knew that it was time to continue the journey uphill, or else return the way from which I had come.

Never wishing to follow the same path, I decided to continue upwards in order to go down and find a new route. I dressed languidly, and wondered at what had powers had conspired to shed my clothes. But later experienced a trickle of fear at the thought of carnivores coming out of hibernation along the path into the unknown.

By 15:30 the sun had lost much of its earlier intensity. The blue shadows of the dense forest stretched long, and hazily shifted across the path like a rough sketch in charcoal. The canopy of branches filtered the strong sunlight and plunged me into an ethereal half world once more. The birds became still; the only sounds were the crunch of the snow under my boots, coupled with the beat of a heart forced into the fast rhythm of the high altitude, and the unmistakable feeling that I was being observed. Fifteen minutes earlier I'd gratefully seen a signpost, but in the colder air the snow's texture had turned crisper, deeper and more abrasive as I rose steadily to the mountain top that teased, never wishing to reveal herself fully.

Branches snapped in a flurry to the far right, with hackles raised and camera ready to take my last photo I stepped-up the pace. A huge *capercaillie*, the size of a turkey clumsily shrieked into the blue-black reaches of the pine forest like an enraged diva. I erased my fear of a grisly death in the clutches of a starving bear with a smile, but replaced it with the deep knowledge that I was feeling apprehensive about the absence of a track and the dark forest which lay all around me.

I pressed on, resuming the internal dialogue that had begun in the solitude of the lower slopes. The forest receded, and a snowy escarpment revealed itself in a series of steep rises; each achingly painted in tints of powder blue, lilac, periwinkle and ultramarine.

Zealously sure that I had to go up in order to go down, and with the conviction that trusting in my instinct was teaching me a powerful lesson about life, I pushed on. The path that I'd followed earlier although full of bright sunlight and easy charm had recently taken a turn for the worse, and as my step faltered, so did my faith. The question that I repeatedly posed was either to return through the grim forest and retrace my steps upon the known path, or to trust in myself and continue upwards? Opting to press on, my soaking boots penetrated the frozen crust of ice like caramel on a crème brûlée, with two-thirds of my leg plunging into the luxurious snow below and my blood turning the snow pink.

The next low escarpment revealed a field of snow blasted into vertical furrows by the breath of winter on a clear blue sky. The fear of change and massive exertion turned into wonder as I began to grasp the startling power of the mountain, and to couple my own path in life into the lessons that were being learnt. I reached the summit, saw a signpost pointing downhill to Grindelwald and smiling ecstatically looked out on the best view of the surrounding mountains that I'd ever beheld.

Recipe for Müesli

Be prepared, as any boy scout will tell you.

A huge bowl of Müesli from the hotel buffet helped me to make it up that peak. Earlier, I'd been aware that I'd be taking a pretty big walk, but it was the first time in thirty years that I'd been in the mountains and I was woefully unprepared for where the path would lead me.

I was wild about the cereal; dried fruit and nuts had been soaked in milk overnight making it tender and delectable. The cook had miraculously lightened the mixture with grated apple and placed the big bowlful alongside a wealth of other luxurious breakfast items. But I think that this is all that you need - and a slice of apfelstrudel and crème anglaise when you triumphantly come down the mountain again.

Measure about 500g of fine rolled oats into a large airtight jar or container. Add a mixture of 50g of almonds, hazelnuts and sunflower seed kernels and 50g of a mixture of chia, linseed and sesame seeds - just select your favourites and be creative. To this add 100g of dried fruit such as raisins, sultanas, cranberries and chopped apricots or dates. Mix the müesli with a big spoon and take about 50g of the mixture per person and place it in a nice deep breakfast bowl, add approximately 400g of milk, cover with clingfilm and leave in it the refrigerator overnight to soak. In the morning grate one washed apple, add to the müesli, a splash of milk, stir and get stuck in.

Heather Gartside

About the Author

Heather Gartside was raised in England and educated at art school. She has traveled widely; living and working in London, Paris and Tokyo. After a successful sojourn as the global merchandising manager for Louis Vuitton in Paris, she then travelled further to live in Belgium, Norway, the, Australia and Denmark. Her work is grounded in different fields: as a writer, a photographer, a teacher and as a designer.

She says: 'Smudging the edges of these disciplines brings vivid painterly elements into the prose and a certain lyricism to images and designs.' Heather currently lives in Denmark with her family.

Rice Pudding in a Duvet is her debut novel. Her forthcoming work, *Into The Middle Distance* once again 'smudges the edges' in combining photography with prose to create a work of magical realism.

MILL HOUSE PUBLISHERS
Stengade 51, D
3000 Helsingør, Denmark
www.millhouse-publishers.com